# GUTTED

A gripping crime thriller full of twists

## EMMY ELLIS

*Detective Tracy Collier Book 1*

**Originally published as *All Those Lies***

JOFFE BOOKS

Revised edition 2024
Joffe Books, London
www.joffebooks.com

First published in Great Britain in 2018
as *All Those Lies*

This paperback edition was first published
in Great Britain in 2024



Cover art by Dee Dee Books Covers

ISBN: 978-1-83526-349-5

# PROLOGUE

If I don't do what I do . . . well, bad things will happen. I don't need any more bad things. Bad things hurt. Bad things make you cry. Bad things . . . are a part of me now. I can't remember when they weren't there. In my life. In my face. In my head. On me, over me, to the point my skin itches with the dirtiness. My hair stands on end if it becomes too much. Like that time when—

*No.*

*No.*

*Please don't make me do that.*

*No more. Please.*

I wish I was out of it. Wish I'd got away like *she* did. She walked. She made something of herself. I bet *it* doesn't bother her now. Like, it's gone, ended, dead, whereas I . . . I'm still here. I wonder if she thinks back at all, to those times, or does she have a clean slate? A clean mind. A clean body.

I want that. Clean — I want to feel clean.

If I do this, I'll be clean. No more bad things. No more of . . . that.

I've dreamt about it so much I've believed the dream. Until I wake up. Here. Until I see the beige curtains, the ones with the holes where moths have got at them. The window they cover is blacked out, painted from the other side. I know it's paint; I've counted the individual brushstrokes a million times. They don't cover the glass thickly. No, only one coat. Just enough so I can't see through it and no one can see in. But I *know* what's on the other side.

I go out sometimes. A lot lately. I wonder why I don't leg it, why I return, and the answer runs away from me. I don't know. Maybe because I love being loved. Even though it isn't right, it's right. *He* told me that.

But I know it's wrong, what he's done, what I've done, and what I'm still doing, but no one would understand unless they've been through it. That love, it does something to you, and even though you hate it, you crave it at the same time. It's all you know — all you've ever known — so it becomes normal.

Still, I'll keep doing what I'm doing, and one day I'll be free.

One day.

# CHAPTER ONE

Copper — and she wasn't called that just because of her hair colour.

Tracy stared at the men in her team. Four blokes, four different personalities, four different ways of caring for her brought to her overflowing table. And, at times, it *was* overflowing. Damn near had her head spinning on occasion. Like now, with them arguing about whether or not they should swoop in on the suspect and bring him in for questioning. As a 'person of interest'. Yeah, right. Whoever believed that phrase?

"For crying out loud." She shook her head, wishing to God she could bash theirs together without getting hauled up in front of the chief over it. Why did they have to be so pushy when an idea gripped them? "We can't bring him in. You *know* that. Not enough evidence. Suspicion alone doesn't cut it. Rather we get what we need and leave him be than move in too soon." She slapped a hand on her desk. "How many times have I said that in the past, eh? And how many times" — she gritted her teeth — "have you lot sodding well tried to overrule me?"

All of them adopted innocent expressions, as though they hadn't stepped on her goddamned toes.

"What, got nothing to say now?" She raised her eyebrows. "I mean, let's just think about doing it your way, shall we? We're close, so maybe we *could* bring him in while two of us question the fucker and the rest of us scramble around trying to find something concrete to pin on him. But what if we don't get anything concrete? It means we have to let him go. And he'll walk, aware we suspect him. Whereas my way . . . Well, he won't have a clue until we drag his arse in here and present solid evidence." She *hmmed*, pressing a finger against her closed lips. "Which one do you think would work better?"

Those expressions again, their wide eyes — two sets of blue, two sets of brown. Stuart, with a red stain to his cheeks, implored her with his eyes to keep him out of this.

"We'll do it your way, ma'am," he said.

She glanced from one to the other in turn. "So kind of you. And the rest of you?"

"Yeah, your way, ma'am," Roger said.

Two more sentences in the same vein followed from Mark and Damon.

And she wondered why the hell they'd even bothered challenging her in the first place.

"Right then." She pointed at Stuart and Roger. "You two stay behind and sift through what we have so far. There's *got* to be something there we've missed." She jabbed a curved thumb in Mark's direction. "And you — you're on phone duty. Chase his records up. I want to know who he's been ringing, when, for how long, and I also want a list of his text messages. Social media, too. Instant messages, daily status updates, photos, the lot. Even how often he goes to the toilet. And you." She widened her eyes at Damon. "You're with me."

He groaned, closing his eyes for a brief moment.

"You may well groan, mate," she said, "but you haven't attended a fresh body in a while. I can't keep giving you special treatment. You puke, you puke, and that's the end of it. No one gives a toss, anyway. Everyone's chucked their guts up at some point. Just a shame you keep doing it, that's all."

Damon took a deep breath. "Can't help it. Something about those scenes get to me."

"Yeah, well . . ." She rolled her shoulders. "They get to me, too, I assure you, but if you let it take over — that feeling or whatever it is — you'd never get any work done." Glancing around at her men, she waited for them to ask any questions. With none forthcoming, she nodded. "Okay. You know what's expected. Damon, come on. The poor bugger we're going to see needs to help us find whoever killed him. Someone's got to give a shit about him, haven't they? Piss poor that the shit comes after he's dead, though."

Christ, she sounded such a heartless bitch. But that was the job for you — and the life she'd led. Hardened you up, gave you a tough outer shell — a tough heart sometimes and all. Still, her attitude and fortitude got results, and that was what the brass wanted. Crimes solved. Job done.

She left the station with Damon in tow and raised her shoulders against the nasty whip of wind that had a mind to slap her senseless. At least it had stopped raining. Pouring cats and dogs earlier this morning, it was. She got into her car and, while waiting for Damon to join her, gunned the engine. She could have done without seeing a dead body herself this morning — not like it was her favourite thing to do, was it? — but murderers weren't in the habit of being considerate. She wondered sometimes whether she ought to walk away from all this, but it would never happen. She'd joined the force for a reason. If she left, she'd go mad with nothing to keep her mind away from things she shouldn't think about.

Damon got in beside her, all whiff of aftershave and that distinct scent of the damp outdoors. He plugged in his seat belt. Glanced across at her. "Why are you putting me through this?"

*His eyes . . . Bloody hell!*

Yeah, he was giving her that look. The one that was supposed to make her relent, to back off from her decision, using the fact he was her lover to get his own way.

*Quite frankly, fuck that, my dear. Work and play are two different animals.*

"Because it's your job." That was all she was prepared to say on the matter. He had to understand that at work, she was the boss.

"And that's it? Discussion over?"

"Yep." She reversed out of her spot. "You've got enough aftershave on to mask any smells coming from the dead bod, anyway."

"Very funny."

"I am indeed."

The start of the journey was made in silence — she couldn't be arsed with chitchat, preferring to go over things in her mind instead. This killer they had their eye on — well, the man they *suspected* of killing random people — was taking liberties lately, murdering one after the other.

All dead in the span of a few weeks. Escalating wasn't the word. And thank God she'd given the order not to repeat to the press or anyone outside the crime team that there was a serial killer out there. If the general public got wind of that, they'd crap a brick. So far, because the victims had come from all walks of life, with no apparent connection, they were being passed off as 'just murders'. But no killing was 'just a murder'. Each one of them was important in its own right, top priority and all that, but the words *serial killer* kind of put the wind up people. A panicking city wasn't ideal on top of what she already faced: nailing the bastard who was doing this.

"Want some company in there?" Damon asked.

She frowned. "Best you don't join me in my thoughts. As you well know, the inside of my head isn't always pretty."

"The outside of it is, though."

She gave him a quick look. "Charmer."

"I try," he said.

"You're trying, more like."

"What's that supposed to mean?"

She imagined him raising his eyebrows. "As in, you're trying. You know, a trial sometimes, a pain in the neck, in my arse."

"You didn't say that the other night when—"

"Aaaand here we are. Crime scene. Work head on — no cock thoughts here, please." She parked then twisted to stare at him. "Remember, deep breath before you see the deceased, turn away if you can't handle it, as though you're searching for evidence around the victim, then come back to me when you've composed yourself. Right?"

He nodded, brown eyes glazing over for a second. "Right."

"It doesn't make you less manly, you know, puking. Makes you human. Makes me admire you more." She got out of the car so he couldn't answer, then strolled over to a PC she hadn't met before and stood beside him at the crime scene tape that had been secured to a few stakes the PC had presumably stabbed into the ground. "DI Tracy Collier. And you are?"

"PC Ben Williams, ma'am."

She smiled, taking in his clean-shaven jaw, blue eyes, and close-cropped black hair. "Well, PC Ben Williams, nice to meet you." She paused, giving their surroundings a quick once-over. "Bit of a way outside the city, isn't it? Still, at least it means the public won't be gawking and getting in the way."

"There is that, ma'am."

Jesus, she hated being called ma'am, as though she were ancient.

"The victim is in that barn there, I heard," she said, pointing a few metres ahead to a dilapidated effort that could once have been called a barn but was now more under the umbrella of broken-down shithole.

"Yes, ma'am."

"Ah, this is Detective Damon Hanks," she said as Damon joined them. "He's with me, all right? Got a log we can sign in to, or hasn't one been set up yet?"

"I did it just before you arrived, ma'am." Williams pulled out a small tablet then handed it to her.

She took it, signed in using the red plastic pen dangling off it, then gave the tablet to Damon. "No one here except you and the other two PCs over there, Williams?"

"No, ma'am."

"Good. I'll see you in a bit." She jerked her head in the direction of the shithole. "Come on then, Hanks."

She ducked beneath the crime tape, cursing a blue streak in her head that she was wearing her sensible flats instead of boots. The ground was waterlogged, and each step she took squelched.

"Fuck's sake," she muttered, almost going arse over tit, her foot sliding on a patch of soggy mud. "If the body was dumped here recently, there'll be footprints. Just a shame there'll be more than one set, what with those coppers over there traipsing all over the place."

"Not their fault." Damon sniffed. "Not like they can fly to investigate, is it? Scenes get contaminated — tough."

"Wow, did you have any actual breakfast with that salt?" She shoved her hands in her pockets.

*Damn cold out here.*

"What?" he said.

Again, she imagined his facial expression. Deep frown, mouth downturned. "Salty. You're salty today."

"Oh, right."

"Got your mind elsewhere by any chance?" she asked. "Because it really should be on the job."

"Nope, fully on the job, ma'am."

Ah, he'd added the *ma'am* as though that would put a prominent full stop at the end of his sentence. As though by saying it, it proved he really was properly on the job. But she knew him — and knew him well — and his mind wasn't properly anywhere. She didn't have time to delve into that business, though. The door to the barn was right in front of them, as were the two PCs standing guard.

"Mitchum, Farrell." She nodded at the blonds then tipped her head towards the door. "Nasty, is it?"

"Fairly, ma'am," Farrell said. "A bit like the one last week."

"I see." She held back a sigh. A large cardboard box sat on the ground beside the door. "Glad to see one of you lot had some sense and brought the papers and rubbers. Time to dress up in our favourite gear, Hanks." She grabbed two sets — paper outfits, booties, and latex gloves — and handed Hanks his. "Best put them on out here."

While they suited up, she studied the immediate vicinity. Footprints — yes, more than one set. Possible drag marks over to the left — the grass was flattened in two distinct channels about a leg's width wide. An old carrier bag — maybe nothing to do with the investigation, but she'd have it collected all the same.

"We'll be off inside, then." She smiled at Mitchum and Farrell, took a step, then stopped. "Oh, Kathy will be here shortly to take care of the victim. She's about fifteen minutes out."

"Okay, ma'am." Mitchum dipped his head once.

She smiled yet again then turned her attention to Damon. She winked to let him know she was thinking of him and what he was about to go through. Didn't want to embarrass the poor bugger by saying anything in front of these two. Although if Damon was sick, they'd find out about his aversion to dead bodies soon enough.

Damon's lips lifted a little, and she took it as a sign he was good to go. Or as good to go as he was going to get, anyway.

Tracy took her own advice. Deep breath. A moment's pause to gather her nerve.

She stepped inside the shithole to see what the killer had left for her this time.

# CHAPTER TWO

Despite the recent rain, the sun was out in full force, its rays creating a slanted rectangle on the concrete floor of the barn just inside the doorway. The light showcased bits of ancient hay, a couple of muddy footprints, and a few cigarette butts that appeared to have been discarded in the last century they were that dried out. They reminded Tracy of crumpled finger bones with faded beige tips. She shuddered, taking a closer peek to ensure they really were just cigarette butts then, satisfied nothing sinister was afoot there, faced Damon.

"Watch you don't tread on those footprints," she said. Why she'd said it, she didn't know — Damon was proficient in police protocol. Force of habit, then, so she never got hauled over the coals for cocking up on the job?

He sighed. "Yes, ma'am."

"You know I can't help it," she said.

"I know."

She inhaled another deep breath. Stared straight ahead at the victim. Blimey, it *was* similar to last week. Guts on display, draping out of a body that had been strung up from one of four rafters still somehow firmly in place. A huge hole gaped in the roof to the left, and the sun found its way in there, too, casting a jagged shape on a bale of hay below and a rusty pitchfork propped against it.

A drying puddle of blood glared at her from beneath the victim's feet, which were about a metre or so off the floor. A lump barged into Tracy's throat. His shoes . . . Worn out, they were, coated in blood, mud, and with holes in the toes. No wonder the deceased had been assumed homeless.

She lifted her gaze and couldn't tell if he *had* been truly destitute or whether his appearance had been made to look this way, what with his hair matted with blood, his face streaked with it, his ragged clothing, too. But that clothing — it seemed deliberately wrecked, like someone had slashed at his burgundy shirt and black jeans. Maybe he'd been someone down on his luck and hadn't been able to afford new shoes.

"Fucking hell . . ." Damon sounded out of breath. Panicked.

"Go away for a minute or two, will you?" she said.

The last thing she needed was to be worrying about him. Maybe she shouldn't have brought him after all. Everyone had lapses of judgement from time to time. In her case, she'd made the wrong call for the first eighteen years of her life.

Damon retched somewhere behind her.

*Bloody marvellous.*

She blew out a forceful stream of air and resumed her perusal of the body. This poor sod might have a family somewhere. Were they worried yet? Had they filed a missing person report already? She couldn't even officially check his pockets — not until Kathy and her team had arrived, photos of him in situ had been taken, then the sometimes lengthy wait for the body to be taken down had been performed.

*Not officially, no.*

Damon had stopped heaving, so she swivelled to check how he was doing. Pale-cheeked, he was shaking, eyes closed, face tilted to the ceiling. He was going through it, then, the shock, the distress, his mind probably working overtime as he tried to process his thoughts and feelings. If he joined her at enough body dump sites, he'd find it got easier as time went by. Her sheltering him from these visuals wasn't doing him any favours, so yes, she *had* done the right thing in bringing him out here today.

"I need some help," she said.

"Oh God. Doing what?" He opened his eyes, lowered his head, and stared straight at her.

"Lugging that ladder over here." She gestured to a free-standing wooden one leaning on the right-side wall.

"You're never going to get him down yourself, are you?" He widened his eyes, and his mouth dropped open.

"No, Damon, I am *not* going to get him down myself. Fucking hell, do I look stupid?"

"No, ma'am."

"Didn't think so."

Damon sighed and traipsed over to get the ladder.

On his return, she said, "Pop it here, away from the blood. I'll just have to lean over, that's all."

He did as she'd asked. "Lean over to do what?"

"Check his pockets. We need ID, and waiting for Kathy and crew to get here would be—"

"What, you can't wait five minutes?" He pursed his lips and narrowed his eyes.

"Patience at work was never one of my strong points, you know that."

"Christ. You'll lose your job one of these days." He shook his head and checked the ladder was steady.

"I expect so, but until that day arrives, I'll carry on as usual."

She climbed the ladder up to halfway and, as she'd said, leant over and slipped her gloved finger into the pocket closest to her, switching her mind off from the fact the body was swaying from her probe. If the killer had done his usual, there would be ID to find. Even knowing their names, finding out their lifestyles, searching their social media and phone records — not one of the dead seemed linked. No rhyme or reason as to why he'd chosen them.

*Maybe there isn't a reason. Maybe he just picks people who are in the wrong place at the wrong time — or the right time for him.*

She touched something and almost whooped with joy. She reached across with her other hand to hold the man still, then dug her thumb into his pocket as well and drew out a brown wallet — relatively new, not something a homeless man would necessarily own. Quickly, she balanced on the ladder while rooting through the contents.

*A driver's licence. Brilliant.*

*Urwin Parks. Hello, you.*

With the arrival of Kathy imminent, Tracy put the wallet back then climbed down the ladder. Damon didn't need asking — he returned the ladder to where he'd found it. Tracy steadied the body so it stopped swaying. She stepped back, surveyed Urwin to make sure he appeared the same as when they'd arrived, and nodded.

"Sorted. No harm done," she said.

"Except you have blood on your gloves and the sleeves of your suit. Kathy is going to know you touched him." Damon grimaced. "Honestly, Tracy, this kind of crap has to stop. You forget I cover for you, keep my mouth shut when you get up to this sort of thing. I shouldn't have to do that." He peered over his shoulder. "And neither should those two out there. What if they saw you?"

A glimmer of guilt fluttered in her belly, soon gone when she told herself the quicker they found evidence against the killer, the quicker she could arrest the bastard.

"Best I take this lot off, then." Tracy strode to the side of the doorway and removed her papers and rubbers. She balled them up, hiding the blood, and tucked the bundle beneath her arm. "There. Stop worrying."

Damon left the barn with her, and they stood outside, Tracy squinting from the sun beaming directly in her eyes.

"Ah, Kathy and the others have arrived." She gave Damon a quick glance — *shh, all right?* — and pasted on a suitably grim expression.

Kathy strode towards them, thin as ever, her black ponytail swinging from side to side. A short, wide photographer trotted behind her, the sun glinting off his bald head and the lenses of his horn-rimmed glasses. SOCO followed, too — two men, lanky, middle-aged, going grey at the temples — their faces showing they didn't relish the job ahead.

Tracy pressed the balled-up wad of paper clothing closer to her body. Maybe she worried they'd spot it, maybe she didn't, but it was too late to feel much of anything now. She'd broken protocol, and that was all there was to it. She'd suffer the consequences later — if and when they arose.

"All right, Tracy?" Kathy asked, stopping in front of her as though a brick wall prevented her going farther.

"Not too bad, considering." Tracy smiled and jerked her head in the direction of the barn.

The photographer and the other officers walked past — Tracy assumed they'd go straight into the barn, getting to work, no messing about. Good blokes, they were.

"It's the same as the others in there," Tracy said. "Guts out and whatnot."

Kathy grimaced. "Bloody hell. This is getting worse."

"You're telling me. Hanks has puked, by the way."

"Now there's a surprise." Kathy smirked. "He needs to toughen up, that one."

"Yeah, well, some people have such queasy stomachs, don't they?" Tracy winked.

"I'm standing here, you know," Damon huffed out. "I mean, you know that, right? So it seems to me you're taking the piss."

"He needs a medal," Kathy said. "You've got a right brainy one there." She gave Damon a sympathetic look despite her ribbing. "Anyway, mustn't stand around nagging with you two, much as I'd like to." She sighed. "Give me a call in a day or two. I should have something for you then, although we all know what I'm going to find. Same killer, same method, no killer DNA or fingerprints, blah blah blah. Christ, is it too early for wine? A whole bottle? Yes? Bollocks . . ." She lifted a hand and trudged off.

Tracy laughed. Didn't feel bad about it, either. Life went on, so they said. And they were right. "Come on, you." She gestured at Damon. "We can nip off for a coffee, if you like. Settle your stomach before we go back to the station. Seems to me you need a breather."

He straightened his shoulders and puffed out his chest, his cheeks ruddy. Anger? Embarrassment? Both? "Enough now. God, some might say you emasculate me on purpose. Not good, Tracy."

She winced at that. He rarely called her out during work hours, and she admitted to herself she'd gone too far by joining in with Kathy's joke — if it could even be called a joke. Tracy hadn't stopped to think that Damon might not find it funny — that they'd acted like bullies.

"Shit. Sorry," she said. She meant it, too. The last thing she wanted was to offend him — whether he was her lover or not. Talking down to her staff wasn't her usual style, but something about this case niggled at her, something she couldn't grasp, and it infuriated her, sent her crabby.

"Listen," she said, desperate to lay the blame somewhere other than on herself — she'd taken a lot of blame in times gone by and refused to do it now if she didn't have to. "Kathy turns me into someone I'm not — she's got a knack of changing me, always has since we were at school. I won't do it again."

He sighed. "Best you don't, eh? It isn't nice, love. It isn't *you.* Not to that extent, anyway."

*Ouch.*

"No, I imagine it isn't nice." Her face heated. Prickled. "Honestly, I feel bad. I'll make it up to you, I promise, all right?"

He nodded. "Yeah. Come on. I want that coffee you mentioned."

They picked their way over the field, ducked under the tape, then signed out of the scene. Mitchum had switched places with the other PC and tucked the tablet away then stood with his hands behind his back, typical copper-on-watch stance.

"You know where I am if you need me, Mitchum."

"Ma'am." He dipped his head, then, chin up, perused the distance.

She wondered what he was thinking — *who* he was thinking about. Did he have a wife or husband at home? Kids? Dog? Picket effing fence? All the things Tracy wanted but didn't think she deserved?

*Don't go down that damn road.*

Tracy nodded at Mitchum then led the way to the car. Her shoes were trashed, so she opened the boot, tossed the bloodied papers and gloves to the rear, then pulled out clean footwear. In the driver's seat, she sat with her legs out of the vehicle to remove the dirty ones then swung her legs inside to put on the fresh. "I really am sorry."

He rested a hand on her thigh. Heat seeped into her skin, and she resisted the urge to lean over and draw comfort from a hug, like she would if they were at her place. Or his.

"I know," he said. "Forget about it now."

She nodded, guilt doing a grand number on her stomach, twisting it in knots, as though it wanted to wring every ounce of repentance out of her. She slung her dirty shoes into the back seat — sod the mess it would make — then closed the door.

They sat for a few moments in silence — one that crept around her on eggshells. God, when would she ever learn to keep her mouth shut? No wonder her previous relationships hadn't lasted. She was too much of a bitch. She had to stop treating people like this. Easier said than done, though — wasn't it?

She took a deep breath then let it out slowly. "Listen, I want to change. I *need* to change. I've been trying to for years, but parts of the old me creep in."

"I love you as you are." He rubbed her thigh.

She gained comfort from it, but he shouldn't always be the one to do all the running, the caring, every-bloody-thing. She'd hate herself even more at this rate if she carried on thinking along those lines. But she didn't know how to love, not really, so a proper relationship was confusing to her. "I know, but you shouldn't have to put up with me like this. I'm well aware I'm stubborn, come off as too hard, too uncaring, but . . ." She shook her head. Could she say it? "Bugger it."

"You can do it," he said.

She grimaced. "Oh, I love you, all right? There, I've said it."

She dared to gaze across at him, her cheeks far too hot, itching, butterflies creating merry hell in her gut. Having a riot, they were, their wings fluttering madly, as though they wanted her to throw up, wanted her to suffer. As though she needed some kind of punishment for her behaviour. And she did, she acknowledged that, even though it stung like a motherfucker.

He stared through the windshield, a grin all but taking over his damn handsome face. She'd say her heart melted, but that was going a bit too far. She didn't do mushy, never had, but maybe that was the problem. Maybe she needed to learn that being soft-hearted didn't mean she was weak.

*'Don't ever let anyone know you care, Tracy,' her father said. 'Otherwise they'll trample all over you.'*

"I wondered when you were going to say it," Damon said. "Thought you never would, to be honest."

"God, I've wanted to for so long but—"

"I know. You don't have to explain it all again. I get it. I understand. I don't always like it, mind, but there you go. Can't always have everything you want, can you? I care about you, Trace. A lot. That's why I'm still here. Why I haven't called it a day and put in for a transfer. You matter — you're worth sticking around for."

Thank goodness he didn't want her repeating the painful things she'd already told him — her way of explaining why she acted like she did. She didn't want to go down that road, the one called the Past, where memories of *him* stood on the kerb in a rigid line, ghosts intent on bringing her down. He was a rum bastard, her dad. The things he'd done . . .

*Things you've never reported him for, you stupid—*

"Don't," Damon said. "Don't do it to yourself."

"How did you know?" Tears threatened, and she cursed them to Hell and back.

"Because I know you. Know what you do to yourself. Like I said earlier, forget about it now. Move on. Become a new you — still you but a different version, because I wouldn't want you to change too much."

"Oh yeah? So you enjoy my acerbic side, do you?" She jabbed him in the ribs.

"Most of the time, but I'd enjoy that coffee more — if you ever start the engine and drive away from here."

"You sod." She jammed the key in the ignition. The engine grunted to life, and she smiled so hard her cheeks hurt. He was good for her, was Damon, and she'd do well not to mess this up.

"Latte, two brown sugars . . . yeah, that'd go down nicely, seeing as you kept me up last night."

He finally turned his head to face her, his grin wider, a glint in his eyes that told her he'd enjoyed himself with her into the early hours of this morning. She wished they weren't here, that they were at one of their houses, huddled under the covers, a scribble of tightly entwined arms and legs. Yeah, she'd give anything for that.

She secured her seat belt. "You don't think . . . ?"

"No, I don't. My boss shouldn't want me to skip off on the clock."

Tracy smiled. "No, she shouldn't, but she does."

"Come on, get out of here. It'll soon be the end of the shift."

Tracy eyed the clock on the dash. *The end of the shift my arse.* It had only just begun, and with the workload they had, they'd be lucky if they finished at regular hours today.

"Sometimes I wonder why I do this job," she grumbled, shoving the car into gear then driving off towards the road.

"You know why you do it, love."

"Yeah, I do." And she erected a brick wall pretty sharpish to stop the Past entering her mind.

# CHAPTER THREE

The coffee shop bustled with people emitting a cacophony of noise that grated on Tracy's last nerve. Their laughter and conversation seemed enveloped in the scent of cappuccino and Danish pastries, jam and cream, flapjacks with over-cooked oats, the air thick with the combined assault to her senses. Cloying, or 'close' as her mother used to say. The heat from the day didn't help, and with no air conditioning, they may as well have been in a sauna. Sweat prickled her upper lip, and she swiped it away with the back of her hand.

Uncomfortable in her own skin — it itched with the close proximity of other customers — she left Damon to order at the counter and picked her way through the tables to the only empty one left in the corner by the door. The long handle of someone's mint-green baby bag hanging on a buggy snagged on her knee, and she almost went sprawling.

She eventually sat, rage building, trying to force it to retreat. She shouldn't be so volatile all the time, ready at a moment's notice to fly off the handle. There was always a bright side, though — or so people kept telling her. At least from here she had a bird's-eye view of everyone else, something she preferred. Knowing who was coming at you was a bonus in her book. Stood to reason, didn't it, considering her past. If she wasn't fully aware, things went wrong.

Terribly wrong.

*Don't.*

Emotionally mixed up, that's what she was, a smorgasbord of feelings churning inside her that usually pointed to her not facing her demons and shutting them down for good.

To stop herself from thinking too much, she scoured her surroundings — people-watching paid dividends. A few times she'd caught someone doing something they shouldn't just by her idly taking in the area. Lots of young mothers out today, their children either squalling for the sake of it or burbling and grabbing at food. Did she want children? God, no.

Tracy shuddered, suppressing the images of her ever having a baby. She wasn't the type — plus, she didn't have the love to give. It was hard enough loving Damon. Difficult to care about someone else when you didn't have the capacity to care about yourself.

The man in question breezed between tables and chairs as though no obstacles hindered his path. He had grace, something she wished she had. Fluid, that was Damon, and everything he did appeared easy, as though he didn't view the world through the same lens as she did. Well, he couldn't, could he, what with being brought up in the perfect home with perfect parents. And she was glad about that. No one should live the life she had.

"Thanks," she said, accepting the coffee he handed to her.

He sat opposite, his knees touching hers, and wrapped his hands around the tall glass cup. Cinnamon or the like decorated the froth of his drink.

"Decided on a chai tea, did you?" she asked.

He nodded. "Realised I didn't fancy coffee after all."

Hers was super-hot and burnt the roof of her mouth. She winced at the liquid searing down into her stomach. There was her impatience rearing its ugly head again. "So what do you think? You know, about this . . . person we're tracking?"

"Bit too crowded to talk in here, boss." Good old Damon, putting her in her place.

"There are ways of talking without giving anything away," she said, spinning her cup around slowly, pressing her fingertips and thumb to the rim. Chastened by his warning look, she again scrutinised the other customers.

Christ, so many people packed into one place, all with lives, all with secrets, all spending their hard-earned money on overpriced drinks and food. There had been a time when the only place to buy coffee was in a greasy spoon or from the chip van perched at the edge of the Saturday market. But times had changed, and it was trendy to splash images of your hot drinks all over social media — to what, show how well you were doing in life because you could afford to drop a fiver on a beverage?

She shook her head to rid it of banal thoughts — but weren't banal thoughts better than what she and her team faced? Some nutter out there, offing people for what appeared to be no reason? But there *was* a reason, there always was, and she'd bet her last quid it would be something relevant only to the killer — something everyday people wouldn't understand.

*Or to me. I have a feeling this is directed at me.*

A woman rose from her seat beside the counter, chivvying her kids along, leaving the table in a right old shit state, crumbs everywhere, cold drink cartons dented in the middle, straws askew. Coffee bubbles clung to the inside of her glass cup in the shape of the UK. A barista zoomed in and cleaned up the mess, vanishing it away so fast Tracy wondered if she'd imagined the litter in the first place.

Sliding smoothly into a vacant seat there, a bloke hefted his briefcase onto the table and opened the lid. Something about him had the hairs rising on the back of Tracy's neck, despite him seeming like nothing but a businessman visiting the shop while he caught up on some work. Only the top of his head was visible above the briefcase lid's edge, the darkest black hair with the faintest of grey — or maybe that was the fluorescent light creating lies.

Tracy shrugged, about to turn away and face Damon, but the businessman lifted his head a little, showing just his eyes and the top of his nose. He peeked over the lid with piercing blue eyes and, goddamn it, winked at her. Tracy's cheeks flushed — with anger, not embarrassment — and she frowned to show him his gesture hadn't been well-received. Men who pushed sexuality at her or any woman rattled her cage. She shoved away the thought that she'd been staring at him first and he might be winking to show her he'd noticed, letting her know she was being rude.

Those eyes, though, they were too blue, too knowing and, as much as she wanted to break their connection, she couldn't.

"What's got into you?" Damon asked.

Tracy continued their battle of glares and muttered, "Don't look now, but I think we have a potential weirdo on our hands."

"You attract them something chronic," Damon said.

"Seems so. He's staring at me over his briefcase lid but has no coffee, no food."

"Maybe he's ordered a specialised drink and has to wait for it. Not everything or everyone is dodgy, Trace," Damon said.

True. But something wasn't right. The man unnerved her — something not done easily nowadays — and she didn't like the feeling of being challenged by a stranger.

*Maybe he doesn't like being challenged by me . . .*

There was that — she never did find it easy to see things from someone else's point of view. Self-preservation — watch your own back at all times, because there was always, *always* someone out there ready to stab it when you weren't paying attention.

But she didn't want to be the first to break eye contact. Seemed he didn't either. She was saved from having to make a decision by the barista returning, tray held aloft, a coffee and a slice of cheesecake on it. New York, she reckoned, and an expresso, going by the size of the white ceramic cup.

Someone who needed a strong caffeine injection, then, one that went straight to work.

The man snapped his briefcase shut and gestured for the barista to place the tray on top. Tracy couldn't get a good gander at his face — his head was down; maybe he was making eyes at the coffee now directly beneath his nose — and she gritted her teeth in frustration. She clocked his taupe mac covering a grey pin-striped suit, white shirt, and blood-red tie. Clean-shaven, pale cheeks, square jaw, and a large mole to the left of his mouth.

He didn't glance up. Instead, he dug a fork into his cheesecake then brought a piece to his fleshy lips, the lower more bulbous than the top. Seemed he either had chapped lips or someone had smacked him in the mouth. A deep split marred his Cupid's bow, the beginnings of a scab forming.

Tracy shrugged, bored now he didn't want to play 'stares' anymore, and returned her attention to Damon.

"Someone pissed him off," he said, eyeing the bloke. "Nasty cut on that lip."

"Well, if he winks and ogles everyone he comes into contact with, he's bound to get a clout at some point." She shivered, the someone-walking-over-her-grave kind, and sipped her drink, which was cooler now but still warm enough to irritate the burn from her previous gulp.

"Maybe he didn't like *you* staring," Damon said.

"Maybe he didn't."

"Maybe you think it's your right because of what you do for a living — but it's not. You should still follow the social rules like everyone else."

Indignance boiled in her belly. "As well as on your breakfast, did you put salt in your tea instead of sugar, too?"

"You're not funny, Trace."

"Clearly not." She stood, waiting for Damon to do the same.

His words had hit a sore spot, so she purposely didn't take any notice of the peeking man as she exited the shop — she liked proving a point. Damon was a minute or so in joining her out on the path. She couldn't help but spy on the coffee-shop man while passing the huge glass window, though. And there he was, glaring back, his fork pointed towards her, as if in warning. She gave him the middle finger, and his cheeks pinkened, two spots the size of doughnut holes. Anger — she'd riled him — and a perverse part of her was glad. Men like him needed—

*Taking down a peg or two.*

Rolling her shoulders to ease the tension out, and fighting against the uncomfortable tickle of being violated by just a pair of eyes, Tracy led the way to her car, her scalp prickling. Once inside, she waited for Damon to get settled in the passenger seat and read her the riot act — or at least read from the hymn sheet he usually sang from.

"Not every man who behaves like that bloke is your dad, Trace."

Well, she hadn't been expecting *that.* "I know. I can't help it, though. See a man like him, and I go into battle mode."

"He's just some fella out for a coffee, maybe a business meeting. He's not a kiddie fiddler or an emotional manipulator. He's not a gaslighter. He's—"

"I get the sodding picture, all right?" She held up a hand, partially to stop him talking, partially so she didn't see the love and compassion in his eyes. He cared for her too much. It could be his downfall. "Fuck's sake!" She smacked the heel of her hand on the steering wheel. "Again, I'm sorry. I always seem to be biting back at you. I swear I don't mean it — it just . . . pops out before I can stop it."

"I know, love." Damon reached out and rested his hand on her thigh. "Ever considered therapy?"

"Don't you start. I get enough of that crap from my doctor."

"There's a reason therapists exist. They fix people — people like you. Don't you *want* to live a normal life?"

His voice, so gentle, soothed her ire.

"What's normal? Is *anyone* normal? Are their lives?" She'd seen too many fucked-up people. Too many monsters. And she'd learnt *those* lessons early — five, she'd been five when he'd — "Right. Back to the station. We need to do a search, find out as much as we can about poor old Urwin Parks. Maybe we'll come up trumps and discover something that may actually be of help."

"Back to being a copper, just like that," Damon said, taking his hand off her thigh.

"It's how I survive, matey. If I didn't go around in this persona, I assure you, you wouldn't like the real me."

"I would, you know."

"Hmm. Whatever."

She gunned the engine then screeched out of her parking spot, the adrenaline rush of driving too fast chasing away all those creepy little feelings the coffee shop encounter had inspired. Yes, people like that man needed sorting — and she was the perfect, screwed-up person to do it.

# CHAPTER FOUR

"Who was that?" Tracy asked Stuart, who'd just placed his desk phone back in the cradle after a call that had him appearing excited and antsy.

He twisted in his chair to face her, tapping the end of his pen on his desk. His eyes seemed to glitter, and his mouth spread into a smile. "Only someone reporting they saw a car on the road near the barn where the latest victim was dumped. This morning, about four. Said it was odd because when they go to work, no one else is usually out and about. That's why the driver took notice. Reckoned he doesn't see a soul on that road until he reaches the crossroads that leads to the motorway, so it threw him. A Mr . . . uh . . ." He peered at his notebook. "Foldes. Henry Foldes."

"Oh, right. Get a reg number, did he?" She'd bet he bloody hadn't — she wasn't that lucky.

"No — sod's law, right — but it's a Lexus, black, with a pink car seat in the back." Stuart raised his eyebrows. "Mad bastard killer with a kid? I'd like to say that isn't likely, but you know how it goes."

"Don't I just." Tracy sniffed and glanced over at the white board filled with black writing, some red and underlined, and a few images of the victims before they'd been killed. Happy faces, smiles wide, not a care in the world. Nice not to have to be reminded of the state they'd been in when Tracy had gone to view them for the first time. Damon would be puking all over the shop in that case. "So, you know the next step. Search for that type of car. Let me know when you have the full list, will you? I want names, addresses, as usual. Thanks."

She strode off without waiting for an answer. In her office, she flopped into her chair and rested her head back, knowing there would be around three thousand or so cars to whittle down to one. No CCTV out in the sticks, so even that avenue was closed. Dead ends — her working life was full of them.

*Remind me why I chose this profession again?*

Damn it, she knew why — and only three other people did, too. Damon, her mother, and her father. She pondered on why she'd opened up to Damon on that subject. Why him? Why not one of the other men she'd had a relationship with in the past? Maybe because she trusted Damon, had been his partner at work for longer than his partner in bed. And she had to stop thinking that way. Damon wanted to be her life partner, not just some bloke she shagged every other night, had meals with, and watched the occasional movie with while snuggling her head in his lap.

As if thinking of Damon brought him to her, his signature knock of *tap-tap* pause *tap-tap* broke into her musings. He waited a beat, then, when she didn't do her usual "Come in!", he entered and closed the door behind him. By the expression on his face, this wasn't a work-related visit.

"I've been thinking, Trace."

She smirked and swung her chair from side to side. "Always a bad sign. It can get you into trouble."

"Pack it in for a minute — I'm being serious." He sat in the spare seat opposite her, the desk width between them seeming like miles instead of three feet. His black suit jacket crumpled at the hem, and his grey tie curved in the middle, a hill of fabric over a white starched shirt. "What we talked about earlier. The therapist—"

"Uh, no time for that nonsense. I have things to do. I want to do the search on Urwin Parks myself — you guys are overloaded as it is. So, if that's all?"

He frowned, and God, the guilt rising inside her had Tracy wanting to go over to him, cradle his head against her chest, and ask him what she'd done to deserve him. She didn't, though. Didn't fancy becoming undone. Not good when at work, was it, to break down your barriers?

"It isn't nonsense," he said, remaining in his seat, leaning back and getting comfortable. He wasn't going away anytime soon, then. His tie straightened out, reminding her of an insipid tongue. "I'd say it would help with work. You'd get a better sense of yourself, too — instead of pretending to be who you currently are, when I know, deep down, the real Tracy is in there somewhere. Don't you want to find out who she is, to be who you were meant to be before *he* messed it all up? To be reunited with her, for want of a better word?"

Tracy thought about that for all of one second. "No. She's a sad, silly bitch who let things happen to her — and kept letting them happen until she was eighteen. Who does that? Who doesn't go to the police the first chance they get, eh? Her, that's who. The current me knows better — I should have told someone."

"Don't you think conditioning has something to do with why you didn't tell? Don't you think the threats played a part? You know all this from training. Even the most strong-willed people can be forced to do things they don't want to do. And the way he did it, the way he manoeuvred things to his advantage . . . Don't you think—"

"You really don't want to know what I think. Seriously." She took a few deep breaths to steady her thrumming heart, to stop herself from snapping at Damon. She wanted to stop being that sharp person — one of many she'd adopted over the years, wearing them like the latest trendy boots until the shine wore off, the cracks appearing through lack of care, the dirt and grime reappearing no matter how much she tried to hide it. Then she'd reinvent herself all over again — wash, rinse, repeat *ad nauseum*. "Actually, maybe I *should* tell you what I think. Maybe then you'd leave off trying to fix me."

She willed herself to be cruel, to lay it all out for him so he was in no doubt what secrets she held inside.

"I lie awake at night imagining stabbing him. Imagining being the very people I spend my days trying to catch — a criminal. A killer. I think of all the lost opportunities, like the time he posed me on the bed with a sheet across my tits and a red rose on top, then took pictures — those times, when he thought rose petals leading a path into my bedroom where he'd . . . He thought it showed he cared about me."

Damon grimaced. Flushed. Squirmed.

*Not so good when you hear the nasty side of the truth, is it?*

"Oh, there's so much I haven't told you," she said. "Because I don't want to hurt you . . . don't want to live through it all again, but hey, sod it, I'm on a roll now; you've opened up the gates a crack, so be warned, some things will spill out, and you won't like them."

She stood to pace the room, keeping her back to him so he wouldn't see what she knew damn well was on her face — tears, something she didn't like shedding. It weakened her, reminded her of what *he* used to say.

*'Crying is for babies, Tracy, so stop that right now.'*

*'But it hurts, Daddy.'*

*'Love doesn't hurt, sweetheart.'*

*'Then this isn't love.'*

The slap that had followed — it had stung like a son of a bitch — and she'd held her sobs inside so she could pretend it *didn't* sting, pretend that this was love.

Was this the kind of bullshit Damon wanted her to tell him? Was this what she'd have to spew to some therapist — someone she didn't even *know*?

*Sod that.*

"I'm about as messed up as you can get," she said, the carpet fibre blurring as she stared at it. "I'm not your average woman, Damon. You either accept I can't go to a therapist or you can call it quits right now."

"Trace . . ." His voice sounded a million miles away yet right behind her at the same time. "I've made an appointment for you."

"You've *what?*" Bugger the tears. She spun to face him, conscious she was a mess, her cheeks hot, her red hair flying then sticking to her wet cheeks. "How dare you!"

"You've got to face it all one last time," he said, still seated, gripping the arm rests until the ends of his fingers turned red from the pressure.

"I haven't *got* to do anything." She returned to her chair, bringing up the screen so she could search out Urwin Parks. "Not anything like that, anyway. But this?" She jabbed a finger at the monitor. It bent her nail downwards and hurt. "This I *do* have to do. I need to find out who this man was and catch the bastard who did this to him. I have to right wrongs, to make everything good again."

"For other people but not yourself?" he asked. "Don't you deserve justice, too?"

"Fuck you." He was right, but damned if she was going to admit it. How many people had she said the same thing to over the years? How many men and women had she urged into therapy in order to get their lives back on track? Why didn't she matter? Why didn't she deserve the same?

*'You're a worthless piece of shit, Tracy Collier, and don't you forget that. After all I've done for you. I showed you love, didn't I? I gave you more than your average father, and look at all the thanks I get. Go on, leave. Do what you said you'd do. Join the bloody police force and stop others from being loved like I loved you. You've gutted me, girl, and you can go hang for all I care. Go on, get out, and don't ever come back.'*

*'I've told Mum.'*

*'You little—'*

"Fuck you?" Damon said quietly. "Is that all you've got? That isn't the right answer. And as for you saying I should call it quits . . . Never, Tracy. Never." He stood then leant on the desk, fingers splayed. A crumb from yesterday's sandwich peeked between two of them. "You might have given up on yourself, but I'll never give up on you." He straightened, dug two fingers into his suit jacket pocket, and brought out a business card. He tossed it on top of a pile of files to her left. "The appointment time is on the back. Tonight, after work." He shrugged. "This is all the help you need, love. I'm going back out there with the others. See you later."

He left, the click of the door closing so final, cutting through the silence in his wake.

She let the tears fall. Could she do what he wanted? Would it even help? She dreamed of a perfect life, one where her only regret was not dancing at school parties or having a friend over for tea. That hadn't been possible. What if *he'd* taken a shine to one of her friends? What if he'd wanted to love *them*?

No. She'd let him do what he'd wanted to save others.

*But what about when you left? Do you even know what he's been doing since? What if he's—*

*Don't think about it. Block it out like you always have.*

She gripped her hair, tugging until it ached. Teeth gritted, she slapped her hands on the desk, the impact driving pain up her wrists. Urwin Parks. *He* was who needed her now. His family, if he had any, deserved answers.

And that reminded her. She needed to find his address. She possibly had a wife to visit, a woman whose world was about to be shattered by the terrible words Tracy had to say.

"I'm DI Tracy Collier, and this is DS Damon Hanks. Please may we come in?"

# CHAPTER FIVE

I don't think about what I've done. I don't think about the people my actions have hurt. I can't. I have to put it to the back of my head, forget about it, otherwise I might go mad. And I don't want to go mad. If I do, I won't enjoy my freedom when it comes.

I'm allowed out again tonight. I wonder who will be next. What are they doing now? Are they having breakfast, getting ready for their last day? And isn't it weird — they don't even know it's their last day. They'll go to work, maybe, or take the children to the park. They'll make dinner and gather around the table, the whole family sitting together, talking about what they've been up to, trading stories and love. Perhaps their baby is teething. The Calpol has run out, so they need to go to the late-night pharmacy. The little bundle of joy needs pain relief, and the parent will go and get some.

When they're out, they'll meet me. They'll be gutted when they do.

Literally.

# CHAPTER SIX

"Hello, Mrs Parks. I'm DI Tracy Collier, and this is DS Damon Hanks. Please may we come in?" She flashed her warrant card, holding it up so it was easily visible, then tucked it back in the inner pocket of her jacket. It snagged against her phone, and she reminded herself for the umpteenth time to stop putting her mobile in there.

The woman peering through the four-inch gap of her open front door seemed confused, brow furrowed, mouth downturned. She appeared to have been on a bender, suffering from a hangover, perhaps. She clutched her dressing gown with one spindly hand at her collarbone, the fluff of the dirty-white fuzzy material blowing a little in the breeze. Her black hair a bird's nest, she shivered, and Tracy recognised it for what it was — that walking-over-your-grave sensation she always got.

"What do you need to come in for? If Urwin's been caught stealing again, it's nothing to do with me. We're separated, have been for months. What he does now is his business." She scrunched up her face, pewter-coloured eyes disappearing beneath puffy lids that bore the Amy Winehouse kohl flick, a remnant of yesterday's make-up. A stain on her lapel screamed slovenly at worst, accidental spill at best. Tomato sauce?

"It is about Urwin, yes, but it's better if we come in." Tracy straightened her shoulders and, out of the corner of her eye, caught Damon adjusting his tie. He did that when uncomfortable, and she felt for him. No copper liked giving this kind of news. "It isn't advisable we do this on the doorstep."

"For fuck's . . ." Mrs Parks widened the door and moved back, her pink-painted toenails digging into a grotty black carpet runner. "Come in then. But make it quick. I need to get to the shops."

*You're not going to feel like doing that.*

"Thank you." Tracy stepped into the house, glad she had shoes on, and hoped the woman didn't ask her to remove them.

Damon followed, and Tracy checked out their surroundings.

Stairs stood to her left in a narrow hallway, covered with grey carpet, threadbare in the centre of each tread where years of feet had trampled over it. Kitchen to the right, sunlight coming through what she guessed were slatted blinds at the window, slicing across the worktop in bright lines, highlighting crumbs, tea stains, and a crusty fork, a pea on the middle prong. Living room ahead, curtains drawn, a lamp with a wonky red shade sitting on a small table beside the arm of a brown velvet sofa, nothing else in there visible.

The air — it stank of dried piss and old food, the undeniable smell of urine missing the toilet bowl and pizza boxes sitting out for days. That would explain the lapel stain — pizza sauce. The place was unloved. Maybe Mrs Parks had been going through a bad time since her split from her husband. Maybe she'd given up giving a shit. Whatever, the woman didn't need this news today.

She led them to the living room and opened the flower-patterned curtains. Dust motes gusted off the fabric, swirling. An old-fashioned three-bar fire squatted on an aubergine-coloured tiled grate, bringing back memories Tracy would rather stay away. The image of her standing in front of the fire in her childhood home burst into her mind, her crying because love wasn't love and she hurt — God, she hurt.

"Take a seat," Mrs Parks said.

Tracy would, only the sofa and two chairs had other guests — magazines, crisp packets, an ashtray, balled-up tissues — discoloured at that. No, she wouldn't be sitting.

"I'd rather stand, thank you, Mrs Parks, but please, sit yourself down."

*You're going to need it when your knees turn to jelly.*

Mrs Parks frowned, appearing uncertain for a moment or two, then slumped onto the sofa in the middle, a magazine crunching in protest. Damon remained by the door, and Tracy stepped back to stand beside him — unconsciously distancing herself from the woman and her filth? From the emotion Mrs Parks might display?

From the damned three-bar fire?

Shuddering from the Past, Tracy got herself together — she had a job to do, things to find out. "Mrs Parks, when did you last see Urwin?"

"My name's Cheryl. Can't stand being called Parks." She rubbed her forehead with two nicotine-stained fingers. "Erm, last time I saw him. Lemme think." She closed her eyes for a second, her mascara-clogged lashes fluttering. "Last week. Came round here after some money. Bloody tosser. I fucked him off, though, didn't I. Told him he wasn't welcome round here no more. Like, he doesn't get we're separated. Thinks we're just on a break."

"I see." Tracy held back a sigh. "Where was he living? Do you know?"

"Some room or other with one of his mates — or so he said. Can't believe a word that comes out of his gob these days." She laughed, the sound bitter — full of regret for a life truly unlived? For dreams gone down the swanny? Her world flushed down the shitter? "Can't say I believe anything he's ever said now, know what I mean? Bit of a prick is Urwin."

"Do you know if he was in trouble with anyone? As in, was there anyone who wanted to cause him harm?"

Cheryl roared with laughter, displaying a few silver fillings in her back molars, some rotting enamel, too. "Everyone who came into contact with Urwin wanted to cause him harm. He's got the kind of face you want to punch. The attitude to match, and all. Like I said, he's a prick."

Tracy forced herself not to raise her eyebrows. "What did he do for a living?"

Cheryl sniffed. "Well, he dressed up nice, looked the part. People'd think he was a businessman, but he wasn't. Scammer, that's the best way to describe him. He likes getting money out of people then running for the hills. At least that's what I found out he was doing before we split — and that's *why* we split. I'm on the social. Can't be doing with getting that taken away from me if they found out we had other money coming in."

Frowning, Tracy asked, "So, while he lived here, where did you think the money was coming from other than in benefits? Surely you realised your payments wouldn't stretch to fancy clothes."

Cheryl held up her hands, sat forward in her chair. "Listen, I didn't know what he was up to, did I? As far as I knew, we lived off just the benefits. Come to think of it, I should have known he was up to something, what with the togs he was buying. I mean, it's obvious I haven't got a pot to piss in." She gestured to her decrepit dressing gown. "So many things are obvious now." She shook her head. "I just didn't see them at the time because I loved him."

Tracy ran through the information in her head. He extorted money — he could have annoyed someone enough for them to kill him. She didn't need a mob or gang case on her hands, but she'd get the team to poke into that angle later. Maybe the victims were related after all.

"Do you have the name of the person Urwin was staying with?" Tracy asked.

If Cheryl had noticed Tracy's slip of the tongue — past tense *was* — she wasn't showing it. "Yeah, Martin Goodall. Another waste of space if ever there was one. Peas in a pod, them two. Known each other since school. Martin was

Urwin's best man." Cheryl sniffed again. Her nostrils were inflamed, red — coke user?

"Thank you. I'm afraid I have some bad news for you. Is there anyone local who can come and sit with you?"

"Sit with me? What the hell for? Just tell me the news and get going, will you? If he's in the nick, good. Saves me having to see him for a while, don't it."

Tracy inhaled a deep breath, then said, "Cheryl, it is with regret that I have to inform you that Urwin was found dead this morning." Blunt, to the point, but hell, she didn't know any other way.

"What?" Cheryl's eyes bulged, and she grabbed a cigarette from a dented red packet beside her, lit it with a gun-shaped lighter, then sucked. She blew out the smoke, the cloud briefly obscuring the fireplace. "So he's been and done it, then."

"Been and done what?" Tracy's nerves itched — as did her hand. She had the urge to grip that sauce-stained lapel and haul Cheryl to her feet, shake some sorrow into her.

"Topped himself." Cheryl took another drag. Exhaled. "Threatened to do it last time he was here, didn't he. Like, he said life wasn't worth living without me — something along those lines. I didn't believe him — and, mean of me, but I don't care."

Grief took people in different ways, but this response was a first for Tracy. Usually, there was some kind of sad reaction — tears, a scream, a collapse or two. But no emotion other than disinterest?

*Bloody hell. I won't tell her he was murdered. It's obvious she doesn't care.*

"That as may be, Cheryl, but as you're still married, it will fall to you to arrange a funeral — and to formally identify him as his next of kin."

"Me? Why do I have to go and see him? Next of kin or not, he's a waste of space. Used to shag about behind my back, too. Did that bird over the road. Karen, that slapper. So . . . no, contact his mother. She'll deal with all that." Cheryl hefted herself off the sofa. She grabbed a mobile from the shelf above the fire. "Got her number here, if you want it, but she lives in the next block of flats anyway. Thirty-four. Harold House. Stupid names for these places."

Tracy had to leave before she said something she'd regret. "Okay, well, if you're not bothered, we'll be off. Thank you for your time." She'd get the mother's phone number from the database in case she wasn't in when they visited.

She strode from the living room, glad to be at the end of the hallway then out of the front door and breathing fresh air. She felt dirty, tainted by being in that flat. And as for Cheryl's behaviour—

*You're judging again. Would you be bothered if* he *died? Would you?*

"Piss off," she muttered.

"Pardon?"

She'd forgotten for a moment she was with Damon. "Nothing. Talking to myself. Call in to Stuart, will you, and ask him to find out where this Martin Goodall lives. I need a breather. I'll be over there."

She left him to it, walking along the balcony that jutted out in front of all the flats. Leaning on the rusty railing outside number fifteen, she took in the city, the mismatched rooftops, other high-rises pointing to the sky, blank expanses of grass and trees that masqueraded as parks, the odd broken swing and wonky slide hazards for the kids. Things hadn't been this way when she'd been a child. The deterioration had grown worse over time until it seemed the council had all but given up caring.

Tracy sighed. Was this how it would always be? Solving crimes, her fighting to encourage people to make their lives better only for them to throw it back in her face? Cheryl — why didn't she care? What the hell had happened to her to turn her into someone who felt nothing regarding her husband's death?

*Remember, it isn't just you who has secrets. Other people are entitled to have them as well.*

That was Tracy's problem — most of the time, she didn't remind herself enough that there were other victims of a terrible life out there. Other people whose emotions had been shredded to the point they couldn't patch them back together.

"Head clear now?" Damon asked, coming to stand beside her. He rested his arms on the rail, hands clasped, and gazed down.

What did he see? Things in his head or the cracked, weed-riddled patio slabs that impersonated a path?

"Sort of. Suppose we'd better go and see Urwin's mother. Phoned Stuart, did you?" She pushed off the railing and headed towards the stairs at the end — they'd been piss-scented on their way up and would no doubt be the same on their way down.

Damon ran to keep up, striding beside her. "I did. He'll call."

"Right. So, on we go."

"Yeah, on we go."

Tracy gritted her teeth, descending the stairs at a pretty fast pace, breath held, wanting to get away from this block, away from . . . *back then.*

Away from that three-bar fire.

# CHAPTER SEVEN

"The thing with telling people their loved one has died is that you don't expect no one to care." Tracy addressed her team, perched on the edge of Mark's desk, the corner digging into the back of her thigh. Annoying. "From what we've gathered so far, no one will miss Urwin Parks, not even his own mother, his wife, or his so-called best friend. The same with the other victims — no next of kin that we've found, no one to give us an insight into why they might have been killed, except maybe work colleagues. Is it a coincidence that those murdered before Mr Parks had no family? Was it just a lucky guess — or has the killer done their homework?" Frustrated, she smacked her fist onto her leg. "And the method of death — got to be significant in some way. They were all gutted. Does their positioning, their posing after death, matter? One in the living room in front of a fireplace, one in a wardrobe shoved naked into the corner, one hanged in a barn. What the hell are we dealing with here?"

*The fire . . . and don't forget the man in the wardrobe had a scarf over his eyes . . .*

Tracy shook her head. "I don't know, but what about this — those found inside residences. How did the killer get in? What, did they just knock on the door and push their way inside? How did they know no one else would be home apart from the victim? Did they stalk them first?"

Her team stared back at her, their expressions blank. She was just spouting off, she didn't expect an answer.

"We've had one a week so far — on different days but always in the evening — so we can't even determine a pattern. Does this person work random shifts, is that it?" She sighed, frustrated. The familiar sense of drowning in information yet at the same time not enough of it threatened to encompass her.

"Maybe they don't work at all," Roger suggested.

"Hmm. So that doesn't fit with the suspect we've been watching. And to be honest, guys, we don't really know it's him. His car has been seen on CCTV at every location apart from Mr Parks' — could just be a massive coincidence. Unlucky for him to have been seen at those locations prior to the victims being killed, which is why we've been watching him."

"Don't forget, he's a pizza delivery guy," Damon said. "He has reason to be near those addresses."

"Has anyone even checked to see if he had deliveries in those places on those days?" she asked, annoyed with herself for not actioning that search — but she *had* actioned the man being randomly followed on some evenings. "Do I have to prompt you to do *everything*?"

*Be the better person . . .*

*Bloody hell.*

"Right, that's on me," she said, surprised at how okay she was with accepting the responsibility of not being on the ball. "Stuart, do that now, please."

*Christ, we could have been watching this man for no reason whatsoever.*

Since when had she not been one hundred per cent in the game?

Stuart's voice penetrated her thoughts — him talking to the pizza shop manager, no doubt. Tracy castigated herself for all the lost man hours spent following this suspect when they could have already eliminated him from their enquiries.

She lowered her head so her men couldn't see the growing blush on her cheeks. Maybe she needed to take some time off. Mistakes like this weren't acceptable.

"Delivery in each spot except for the barn last night, ma'am," Stuart said.

Grasping at straws, Tracy said, "But that doesn't mean he didn't do it — killing them, I mean."

"It does, I'm afraid, ma'am. He returned to the shop after every delivery — no extra time taken. He made it back in the same time he usually does. One of their faster guys, apparently."

"Bring him in anyway. He might have seen something," she said.

Stuart rose, his sigh one of tiredness and not irritation — she hoped.

"Sorry we messed up, boss," Mark said, scrubbing at his whiskers.

"We all did," she said. "Me most of all. Christ, we've all been working flat-out this year. Anyone remember taking a break since January? No, didn't think so. Listen, when you all get a moment, have a chat amongst yourselves and decide who books holiday and when. I'll work mine around yours. In the meantime, I'm off to my office to prepare some questions for the pizza man." She smiled. "Be nice if he brought some food with him, wouldn't it? Bloody starving, me."

* * *

In the interview room, Tracy said, "Mr Quinton — can I call you William? We've asked you here today to help us with our enquiries. We understand you were in the vicinity of two crimes, delivering pizza, and it would be of immense help to us if you can cast your mind back to the evenings in question to see if you recall anything odd." Tracy slid a sheet of paper across the desk with the dates and locations of death on them. "For the tape, I have shown Mr Quinton item number sixteen A — the dates and times of the crimes. Mr Quinton?"

He stared at the page, his sallow cheeks hanging below his jawline, his strawberry-coloured nose getting riper by the second. Shaking his head, he raised it to look at Tracy. His eyes, watery and red-rimmed, told her the shock of being brought in for questioning had manifested itself as tears. "I always go to number twenty-three in Gains Street. Some young lads live together — think they might be brothers — and they're always ordering pizza. Every night sometimes. They usually have a bottle of Coke and all. Nice lads. So, yeah, I remember delivering to them, but the trouble is, because it's most nights, how am I going to remember *which* night I saw something odd?"

Tracy's skin goosebumped. "So you do recall seeing something odd, then?"

"Yeah. Bit of a commotion, by all accounts. I was getting out of my car, see, and this girl was having a barny with some fella on the path in front of a house, in the garden. Seemed like a lover's tiff to me. Shouting and all sorts, they were."

"All sorts?" Tracy willed the man to remember everything.

"Well, she was scratching him, hitting him, telling him love meant she had to do this."

Her nape prickled with sweat. "Excuse me?"

Mr Quinton shrugged. "I dunno, do I. That's what she said. Anyway, the bloke said: Leave me alone, you fucking freak, I'm sick of seeing you out here."

"Then what happened?"

"She went down on her knees, didn't she, all weird-like, begging him to let her in. Come to think of it, it was a house a few doors down from where I was delivering, and the next night, when the lads wanted pizza again, one of them — the older one, had a beard, brown hair, blue eyes, just in case you need to know — he said the bloke who'd been arguing with the girl had been bloody murdered!"

"Mr Quinton, have you ever delivered to that 'bloke's' house before?"

"Can't say I have. He didn't strike me as the pizza type. The times I saw him, and that night, too, he was wearing sports gear and carried one of those bladders."

"Bladders?" Tracy frowned. What the hell was he on about?

"You know, them sports bags that have a pouch in them for water. Runners suck the water through a tube. Saves them carrying bottles. I know this, cos my son has one."

"Right . . . Moving on, Mr Quinton. Was that the only odd thing to occur while you delivered pizza that night?"

"No. I haven't got to the odd bit yet." He sat up straighter and tapped the date on the paper with a podgy finger. "After she dropped to the path on her knees, the bloke went inside. Slammed the door pretty hard. Anyway, I left the pizzas with the lads and returned to my car. I was rolling a ciggie for the drive back, when bugger me, the girl came and stood by my window. Fair shit me up, it did. Not ashamed to admit I jumped and dropped my fag in my lap. Good job it wasn't lit, that's what I say. So she's staring at me, and her eyes were bloodshot, like she hadn't had no sleep. I rolls down the window and asks her what she wants. She said, and I shit you not: Have you ever been gutted?" His face paled. "I'm telling you, it was well off. Like she wasn't right up here." He tapped his temple. "I got that window up pretty sharpish, I can tell you, and drove off."

*Gutted . . .*

"I see. So, did you tell anyone about the incident?"

Mr Quinton nodded. "Yeah, told the others about it back at the shop during a quiet spell. We had a laugh about it, but it wasn't funny, not really. Think I had a bad dream that night."

"Okay. Do you recall anything odd about the other night in question?"

"Do I ever. I only saw her again, didn't I. Yeah, she was hiding behind one of them big wheelie bins — the green ones — outside a block of flats. I'd just delivered to that address on the page there" — he jabbed at the words again — "and was returning to my car, when up she pops. Just her head, mind, above the bin lid."

*The man in the coffee shop staring at me over his briefcase lid . . .*

Tracy suppressed a shudder. "Did she interact with you at all that time?"

"Yeah." Mr Quinton rubbed his arms — the hairs on them stood at attention. "She said: You didn't answer my question before. Have you ever been gutted?" He closed his eyes briefly and inhaled a long, deep breath. "I've gotta say, she shit me up again. Like, she's not normal. Why ask someone that sort of question, eh?"

"I have no idea, Mr Quinton. What happened next?"

"I legged it to my car — wasn't hanging around to see what she'd say or do. And she chased me. Quick on her feet, she was. She reached my car just as I'd got in and was about to close the door. She held the door open by holding on to the top of the window bit, and I couldn't very well close it with her fingers there, so I asked her to leave off."

"And did she?"

"No. She leant in, said: Do you *want* to be gutted?"

"What was your response to that, Mr Quinton?"

"Well, I said no, of course, then I grabbed her hand and threw it off, and I was out of there. I nosed in my rearview, and she was just standing there, in the middle of the road, staring after me. Gave me the willies and no mistake. I told the others back at the shop that I didn't want to deliver to those addresses again if I can help it. Shame, because the lads at the other place give me tips every now and then. Helps buy my tobacco."

"I'm taking it you remember what she looks like, yes?"

"I'll never forget her."

"Would you mind staying here for a while with a sketch artist?"

"Nope, I don't mind. Anything to help." He clasped his hands and cracked his knuckles. "'Ere, you're not telling me she's the sodding killer, are you? Cos I heard someone else was also murdered in the street where she hid behind the bin . . ."

"I'm not at liberty to say anything at this moment in time, Mr Quinton, but the information you've given us is invaluable and very much appreciated." Tracy rose, her back aching, and she longed to pop out the kinks. "I'll arrange for you to have a cup of tea brought in — or coffee, if you prefer — while you wait for the artist." She walked to the door. "Oh, and your car. Is it parked at your address?"

"Yeah, in the garage. Why?"

"I'll need to send someone round to fingerprint it. The window, where she touched it."

"Ah, that might prove to be a problem," he said.

"Why's that?"

"I took it into the carwash the other day. One of those where it scrubs and waxes. I parked under a tree, and a bird crapped all over it."

*Fuck*. "All right. Well, we'll print it just the same. You never know."

# CHAPTER EIGHT

Once again in the main office, Tracy faced her team. "Nuts as this sounds, I think we might be on to something here. It's a long shot, but we could be dealing with a female killer. If she *isn't* the killer, she's definitely in need of help, so we should find her regardless. Mr Quinton had a couple of strange occurrences involving a woman. You'll be able to view the video tapes to watch the interview and hear what he had to say. Now, he's currently in with the artist, and as it's—"she checked her watch — "way past five, I say we call it a day and start again in the morning. We should hear back from Kathy soon about Mr Parks. We all have a good idea how he died, but she might find something else that will help us. So, have a good evening, and we'll meet up here bright and early at eight, ready to do this all over again."

Stuart, Mark, and Roger busied themselves turning off their computers and gathering their personal items. Tracy watched them with envy — they all had good women at home, lovely lives, the three of them happy with their lot. Although a little jealous, she didn't begrudge them. They were fine officers, fine men, and deserved all the good life had to offer.

"Before you go, ma'am." Damon smiled, still leaning against his desk where he'd been during their catch-up meeting. "Don't forget you have an appointment later."

She glared at him, daring him to say another bloody word. He remained silent, thankfully, and she flounced into her office, her intention of going home thrown out of the window, her anger at him trying to force her to do something against her will pinning her to her desk chair. She'd do some paperwork — she'd show him she wouldn't be bullied.

The main office door banged three times — three men leaving separately, or had Damon also left at the same time as one of the others? She didn't much care. She wasn't in the mood to see him tonight — or right now if he'd stayed behind.

*Tap-tap*. Pause. *Tap-tap*.

"Bloody hell," she muttered. "Come in only if you're wanting to discuss the case."

She waited, breath held, for him to enter. Instead, his muffled footsteps on the blue carpet tiles told her he was walking away. And so he should.

She swivelled her chair to the left to pick up the stack of files awaiting her attention and spotted the business card Damon had placed there earlier. Gritting her teeth, she swiped up the card and, legs pistoning, she stalked to the bin and threw it inside. The cleaners would be here around six, and they could take the damn thing away with them. She didn't need a therapist. What she needed was to be left alone — for the Past to be left alone, locked away inside her head where it couldn't get out.

Damon's words flooded her mind. *Did* she want to remain as she was, a parody of the person she would have been had *he* not loved her? *Was* there call for her to spill her guts — *Have you ever been gutted?* — and get everything off her proverbial chest? *Would* a stranger know how to fix her, take away her nightmares, her fears, her absolute disgust with her former self? Her disgust with *him* — and, if she were honest, her mother, who'd maybe known all along? She'd claimed she hadn't — of course she had — but who *didn't* suspect something was going on when a father spent more time than necessary in their daughter's bedroom? Hours. Long into the night.

Tracy sighed, the exhalation shaky, and God, she hated that. A shaky breath meant she was afraid, unnerved, not in control. Like back then.

"Oh, for Pete's sake," she shouted. "Once. I'll go once, Damon Hanks, and then you can get off my back about it."

The main door slapped shut.

He'd gone, then.

She stood, her legs wobbly, and shuffled over to the bin. She took out the card — *Dr George Schumer, Therapist* — and turned it over. Her appointment was at six-thirty. What kind of doctor was he to allow someone to make an appointment on another's behalf? Who in the hell *did* that? Well, she'd soon find out. And she'd give him a piece of her mind while she was at it, too.

Tracy left her office, pleased Damon wasn't loitering in the main room, ready to pounce and cajole her into doing more of what he wanted. Maybe she ought to look at this as her doing something for him instead of him always doing something for her. He cared about her well-being, she understood that, but to make an appointment with a sodding shrink? And to want to stay in a relationship with someone who needed one?

He was something else. A glutton for punishment.

*Or maybe he really does love you.*

She stormed through the building, waving to those at the desk instead of nattering with them like she usually did. She wasn't in the mood for idle chitchat. No, she was in the mood for a good argument, and Dr George Whatever would be the perfect verbal sparring partner.

In her car, she shoved the seat belt on then roared out of her parking space, getting more annoyed by the second. If she smoked, she'd have at least five cigarettes planted between her lips, sucking on them until she choked. Or maybe a bottle of vodka would do the trick. No, that never worked. That particular drink brought the demons out to play — and it seemed they didn't need any extra encouragement. The bastards had been niggling at her ever since these recent murders had started.

She arrived at the doctor's office without remembering how she'd got there, one of those journeys that passed by without her knowledge. She told herself off for not paying attention — she could have caused an accident — then concentrated on what she was doing. Parking in front of a bay window she assumed belonged to the reception area, she eyed the dash. The clock read six-twenty, green numbers bright. Enough time to gather her thoughts, prepare her speech, and get herself under control.

Fat spatters of rain plopped on the windshield, resembling clear splotches of blood from castoff, forcing her out of the car earlier than she wanted. She ran to the building's door, ducking under the overhang just in time. Rain really lashed down then, so hard it bounced off the tarmac and the concrete walkway leading to the entrance. Stair rods, Damon called them.

Tracy took a deep breath, pushed the door, and stepped inside.

This had once been a house, that much was certain. A set of stairs to her right, a door to her left, and ahead, at the end of the short hallway, what she surmised had been a kitchen. She aimed for it, for the door with a frosted glass panel in the top and the word RECEPTION in dark grey. Tapping on it lightly, she waited for a response. With none forthcoming, she boldly entered to find herself in a room with two plush turquoise sofas, a large, kidney-shaped desk finished in pine Formica, and a woman sitting behind it — blonde, blue-eyed, red talons, and silver hoops the size of CDs in her ears.

Tracy cleared her throat.

The woman looked up, her expression showing her disinterest in Tracy — which matched how Tracy felt about her. It was the end of the day, but come on, a smile wouldn't have hurt. Tracy gave her one.

It wasn't returned.

"I have an appointment with Dr . . ." *What was his name?*

"Schumer. Yes, you're his six-thirty?" The woman's voice . . . pure nails on a chalkboard. Her smile left an aftertaste similar to stevia. Dry. She glanced behind Tracy into the hallway, frowned, shrugged, then stared blankly at her desk.

"Yes," Tracy managed.

"If you'd like to come with me?" The blonde stood, smoothed down her black skin-tight skirt, then minced across to the door on heels too high and way too cerise.

*How she suffers wearing them I'll never know.*

Blondie led the way to the door opposite the stairs then knocked — the same knock as Damon's. Tracy's heart panged. She should have asked him to come with her.

"Enter."

Blondie opened the door halfway, popped her head around it, and said, "Tracy Collier for you."

"Ah. Right. Send her in. Thank you, angel."

Appalled by his familiarity in the workplace, Tracy was about to say something when Blondie turned to face her, and her name tag blared ANGEL, black letters on silver.

"He's ready for you now," Angel said, her cheeks flushed, sweat beading her upper lip.

"Um, thanks."

The woman strode away, and Tracy followed her with her gaze. It was clear the receptionist couldn't wait to get home. She stuffed a phone in her bag, slung the strap over her shoulder, and tottered past Tracy to the door, heels tapping an annoying beat.

Unsure how to play this — go into work mode, where she could cope with anything, or be one of her other personas — Tracy took a couple of seconds to compose herself. Then she entered as DI Collier, the no-nonsense woman who didn't take any crap.

Dr Schumer sat behind a vast mahogany desk at the back of the room, looking for all the world like a regular doctor, minus a stethoscope dangling around his thick neck. Suit. Shirt. Red tie. Hair, dark, possibly with speckles of grey, but that could be the fluorescent lighting creating lies . . .

*Christ. The man from the coffee shop.*

What were the odds of that? And it was definitely him — that mole beside his mouth, those piercing blue eyes, and that wink — again. Where did this bloke get off doing shit like that?

"Uh, this isn't going to work out," she said. "Sorry to have wasted a time slot."

"Miss Collier — wait." He rose, pressed his fingers on that damned briefcase of his sitting on his desk, and held out his free hand. "Please, take a seat, won't you?"

She didn't want to take a bloody seat. She wanted out of there, to be at home, guzzling some wine and tucking in to pizza — all that talking with Mr Quinton had given her a craving. Except she was here. But wouldn't it be interesting to spend some time with this man? To ask why he thought it was okay to wink at people the way he did?

Tracy stepped forward and shook his hand — firm grip, dry palms, blunt-ended fingers — then plopped herself on what she assumed was the client's chair, a puffy red recliner — and no, she wouldn't be sprawling back in it, exposing her eternally damned soul.

"My partner, DS Hanks, made this appointment," she said. "Tell me, since when is that ethical?"

"Oh, I'm sorry, is he not with you? I assumed he was using the toilet upstairs. He made an appointment for you both."

"He did?" *Then didn't sodding show. Crafty git.* "Right, well, I wasn't aware he was supposed to be joining me." She blushed with anger, reduced to feeling five years old under his intense scrutiny.

"You're welcome to stay regardless." He moved from behind the desk to a sideboard where a Tassimo coffeemaker sat on top beside a silver filigree bowl with individual creamers and packets of brown sugar poking out of it. "I have decaf if you prefer. English breakfast tea. Chai."

Why not? A sit down and a coffee wouldn't hurt, would it? She didn't have to open up to him. She could have a chat, leave, and never return. Oh, and give Damon what for, too. Tell him that not showing up with her after booking a two-person appointment under false pretences just wasn't on.

“Please,” she said, managing a tight smile. “That would be nice. Strongest coffee you have. Thanks.” She paused, thinking, then, “Can I ask, how did he know about you? DS Hanks, I mean.”

“Oh, the coffee shop. I dropped some of my business cards, and he was kind enough to pick them up as you were leaving. He kept one and called not long after, as I recall.” He inserted a pod into the machine, placed a black cup beneath the spout, and pressed a button. The machine burst into steamy, gurgling life, the aroma of coffee oozing into the air.

“About that coffee shop.” Tracy sat back and crossed her legs, the seam of her jeans chafing on one side of her knee. Irritating, but if she repositioned herself, he might take it to mean she was on edge. Fidgety. And she wasn’t. She really wasn’t. “I considered you exceptionally rude, staring at me like that over your briefcase — and winking.”

Her coffee was done, and he walked over and handed it to her. She took it, annoyed her hands shook, and nodded her thanks.

“And I considered *you* rude to be staring in the first place,” he said and gave her what she termed a sarcastic, arsehole’s smile. “Which is why I decided to mess with you and stare back. Forgive me. I shouldn’t have done it. But, you know, I’ve studied the human mind for so long that I love seeing people’s responses to unwelcome behaviour. I like trying to work out how they tick. Imagine my surprise when Mr Hanks telephoned and asked for an appointment. I admit, you intrigued me from the get-go, so having you here is a pleasure. You could call it a dream come true.”

*Come again?*

He returned to the machine and set up his own coffee.

“So, you want to know what makes me tick, do you?” she asked, well and truly pissed off — and, she’d admit grudgingly, ill at ease.

“Something like that.” While his drink spluttered into the cup, he added sugar. “I’m sorry, would *you* like sugar?”

"No, thank you." Again with the tight smile. Why had she agreed to stay?

"I'd ask if you were sweet enough, but it's evident you're not."

*What did he just say?* "I beg your pardon?" Indignance coated her words, and she had a hard job not getting up and walking out.

*Ride it out. Let him dig himself into a bigger hole.*

"Oh, come now." He really was smarmy, rubbing his hands together like that then seeming to remember what he'd been doing and stirring his drink. "You're spiky; you have an axe to grind, as it were. You'd love to be sweet, but unfortunately, life hasn't dealt you the saccharine card. More like vinegar or lemon. Sharp and acidic. Correct?" He removed his cup from the machine and, opposite to what she'd thought he'd do, he sat on a chair in the bay window, another recliner, dark green leather, gold studs on the arm risers.

Should she admit he was right? Bugger it. "Okay, what else do you sense about me?"

"You've had a traumatic life—"

"Ha! Hasn't everyone who comes here?" God, he was like a fake psychic, blurting out a spiel he'd undoubtedly used a hundred times before.

"No."

*Oh.* "Carry on."

"You can't let anything go — and I mean anything. So, when you next see Mr Hanks, I suspect you'll go for the jugular and ream him out for booking this appointment for you both then not turning up, leaving you to deal with it alone. And you won't just tell him off once, you'll bring it up time and time again in the future."

"And?" If she blushed any hotter . . .

"You want to be loved, but that word — love — it burns a hole in your gut every time you hear it, every time you say it, because love doesn't mean love to you. It means something else."

"All right, so Hanks has been talking." *I'll bloody kill him.*

"No, he hasn't. But someone has."

"What?" Her stomach somersaulted. Nauseated, she stood abruptly, her coffee sploshing over the rim of her cup and burning her hand. She welcomed the pain. "Who have you been talking to?"

"That I can't tell you. Client confidentiality."

"Even you telling me this doesn't sound ethical. How the hell do you know who I am besides my name? I could be anyone. Whoever's been talking to you — and they must have a screw loose to come and see you in the first place — shouldn't have given you my name."

"They didn't."

"What then?" Rage built in her chest, and she placed her cup on the sideboard on top of a coaster, unable to trust herself with something hot, something that could burn a doctor's face. "What?"

"I've seen your picture. I know the other side of your story, so to speak." He calmly sipped his drink, steam curling up and gauzing his eyes.

She shook her head. "No. No, you absolutely should *not* be telling me this. I should report you. It isn't right, what you're doing, what you're saying."

"Are you going to storm out?" He cocked his head. "Isn't that what you usually do when you can't handle something? I don't think you will. You're compelled to know what *I* know — to know the other person's point of view. You'll stay, you'll sit, and you'll tell me your tale at some point, and I . . . will try to fix you. Do you know, it's been a few years since he was here, and I always wanted to mend the girl he broke. Won't you let me?"

*He'd* been here? Talking about her? Telling this . . . this man all their secrets and what they'd done? What *she'd* done?

Tracy glared at him. Then, as he'd mentioned, she did what she always did when the going got tough. She walked out.

# CHAPTER NINE

I'm lucky. The pizza man is over there, standing at someone's yellow front door — nasty shade, that — not a million miles from where I live. I shouldn't shit on my own doorstep, not really, but isn't this the easiest one to pick?

It is.

He fell into my lap, like fate had played her part.

God, I'm so lucky.

He's bigger than me, that pizza bloke, but it doesn't matter. Even the strongest person's gut rips the same once a knife goes into it. Even the beefiest of men drop to their knees, clutching their stomachs, and gaze up at me with *that* question in their eyes:

Why?

Because . . . because this is what love is. Love hurts, even though *he* says it doesn't, and doing this, *being* this person — yes, it hurts. I'm the product of such love, my actions and thoughts determined by that first night, that first creak of the floorboard that told me someone was outside my bedroom door. I'd thought it was Mum, come to tuck me in, then remembered she'd said I was too old for stories now and could read to myself until nine o'clock. But someone had been there. Someone had come in. And my life had changed.

I stifle a laugh. Wouldn't do to become hysterical in public. I shouldn't want to laugh at my life, at what I've been through, but laughter is the best medicine, isn't it? Along with a cup of tea, which cures all ills and worries, and I'll have one once I get home. Earl Grey. Makes me feel posh, that does.

I cut the mirth short. I don't want to draw attention to myself. So why, then, did I approach the pizza man twice before? A glitch, that's what it was, a flicker in my wiring that sent me towards him, even though I knew it was wrong.

He's a witness. He's seen me two times — both by the homes of those I gutted.

He can't be allowed to live.

There he is, walking back down the gravel path, black boots scrunching, his silly company cap pulled low, as though he's hiding his face from someone. Me? Maybe, maybe not.

"Help!"

I sounded pained then, as if someone had hurt me.

Pizza Man tilts his head to one side, listening — waiting for another cry? I give it, more fearful this time, ramping up the urgency, and he jumps, glancing left then right, then to where I'm standing behind someone's front garden hedge — a tall one, taller than me. Taller than him.

"Who's there?" he calls.

*Me, the one who wants to show you love.*

I giggle. I'm mad, I think, sent that way from years of being—

"Oh . . . God, someone help me. Please . . ." I gurgle a bit; you know, to make it more authentic, then smother my mouth with my hand to stop hilarity spilling.

*His guts will be spilling in a minute.*

Pizza Man shuffles over, unsure, I can tell, his body language screaming that he doesn't want to be in this situation, within my grasp — except he doesn't know it's me here.

Yet.

"Uh . . . I can't . . . I can't breathe . . . Help . . . Me . . ."

He's there, on the other side of the hedge, partially visible through gaps in the leaves and branches. Royal-blue polo top, the pizza shop logo on his left breast, some cartoon slice of pizza, pepperoni and cheese on top of tomato sauce. Blue baseball cap, same logo above the peak. Black trousers, his stomach ballooning over the waistband. He's going grey — and I wonder, was he let go from his office job, and all that's left is this one, delivering food to the city's greedy, lazy bastards who can't be bothered to cook their own food?

*You're judgy.*

*Deal with it.*

*Piss off.*

"Who's there?" he asks, voice trembling. He sounds like a little kid.

"Me," I say. Stupid answer — one that has me wanting to laugh *again*.

*Stop it. Control yourself.*

*Yes, ma'am.*

*Grow up.*

*No.*

"Who's me?" he asks. Is he trembling?

"Me!"

I crouch, knees sinking into the damp, cold earth beneath the hedge. Someone has recently turned it over. To plant flowers? Oh, who gives a toss?

The blue of his uniform flickers on the other side — he's moving, walking to the path. Then he rounds the hedge and stands there, staring into the darkness — no lights shine from the house, and the nearest streetlamp is metres away, its glow ineffectual here. Perfect, so perfect. The gods are smiling down on me.

Shame they didn't do it years ago.

"I've been attacked," I say, panting, really getting into the spirit of it all. "Someone . . . someone tried to rob me."

"That your house?" he asks. "Anyone else home?"

"No, I'm alone. I live by myself. Please, help me up."

He comes closer, reaches out a hand for me to take. I grasp it, curling my fingers tight, and he pulls me standing. I lurch into him — and so does my knife — then I jerk it up, back down, my wrist strong from years of—

*Don't.*

He doesn't make a fuss or a sound. But he does slump, which ensures the knife rips upwards again, hitting bone. A rib. Not prime, though. Oh, the things I think.

I slide the blade out and, while he crumples onto the grass belonging to Mr and Mrs Perfect of Holden Lane, in the foetal position, his face a muddy black in the darkness, his teeth and the whites of his eyes the only things truly visible, I wipe the knife on my black trousers then slide it into the scabbard inside my waistband.

Always be prepared. No one wants to walk around with a knife in full view.

"What . . . why . . . ?" he asks.

I pull my phone out of my pocket and select the torch app. Phone beneath my chin, light beaming upwards, I lean towards him and show him my face, wondering if I resemble one of those demonic fuckers who scare people on Halloween.

I grin. "Remember me?"

"Oh . . . Oh God, no. Not you . . ." Blood trickles out of his mouth, meandering — what a great word — down his chin to disappear into the collar of his delivery man's top. "What have I ever done to you?" he splutters, as does the blood, coming out in a misty spray.

He'd better not get any on me.

I sigh, annoyed I have to explain. "You didn't answer my question — twice. You saw me where I shouldn't be — twice. And here you are again. Are you following me? Are you a stalker disguised as a pizza guy?" I pause. His nostrils flap where he's desperate to draw in air. "Tell me . . ." I lean as close as I dare now the blood has stopped acting like a damn geyser. "Have you ever been gutted?"

Laughter *does* burble out then, and I cover my mouth to keep the majority of the sound muffled. The noise reminds me of being a child, trying not to giggle when playing hide and seek. That was so long ago, but that laugh, it brings it all back. I laughed like that before . . . before . . .

I didn't laugh much after that.

"I don't understand," Pizza Man manages.

"No, people rarely do. You have to live it to get it. Be glad you didn't live it. Love hurts, right? A bit like your stomach, really."

I never thought I'd grow up to be like this — uncaring, flippant, a bitch of the highest order. But I am, and I must deal with it. One day, when *he* says so, this will all be over. I'll be able to walk away — blood on my hands, yes — but free just the same. Even in prison I'll be free.

"I need to shut you up now," I say, and the phone torch winks out, leaving only the glow of the home screen to light my way.

Pizza Man rolls onto his back, blood foaming out of his mouth, bubbles, so many of them, reminding me of Fairy liquid in the washing-up bowl. It pours from his midsection, soaking his daft uniform. I'll put him out of his misery, shall I?

A quick slice to his neck sees to that, and then, once I've posed him just right, I'm on my way, whistling.

Four down, six to go.

# CHAPTER TEN

Tracy drew to a screeching halt outside Damon's house and cut the engine, yanking the keys out of the ignition and cursing a blue streak when one of the other keys scratched the back of her hand. A faint line of blood bloomed into several beads and threatened to spill into rivulets. She sucked her skin, the taste of pennies coating her tongue, and remembered another time she'd tasted copper.

The slap had stung, her head flung to the side after the strike. She'd refused to be 'loved', and *he'd* lashed out, incensed at her disobedience, her *spurning* of him, as he'd put it.

"Spurning, my arse," she muttered, pressing down on her hand with the other to stop more blood spilling.

Determined not to think about *that*, she got out of the car, slammed the door, then locked it with the key fob on her way up the garden path. She rang the bell — pressed her finger without pause so the jingle went on and on — and jumped when Damon opened the door.

She stormed into the house, angrier than she'd ever been, and that was saying something. Oddly, not wholly at Damon but at Dr Fuckface, the man who'd told her things he shouldn't have and stirred everything up inside her — in her heart, her mind, her body. Her fucking *soul.* No one had the right to force someone to face things they weren't ready to face — and she could put Damon in that category, except she'd gone to see the doctor of her own volition in the end. All right, Damon had initiated it, but still, she had her own mind, and she'd chosen to go.

More fool her.

"Good evening to you, too, darling," Damon said.

She ignored him, the sound of the front door closing bringing on a wince — the slam loud, far too loud — and stalked into the kitchen, to his fridge, pulling out a bottle of white wine. Rooting through his cupboard, she took out a long-stemmed glass and, with a speed that frightened her, she poured and downed a big helping within a matter of seconds. Frightened? Yes, because this need for alcohol wasn't normal for her. It didn't fix things — never had, never would — and to *need* it as much as she just had . . .

"Good evening, Damon," she said. "*Darling.* There. Better?"

*Why am I such a bitch?*

He knew not to roll his eyes but came close, sighing as though she wore him out and he was tired of her. She wouldn't blame him if that were the case — she got on her own nerves half the time. Scrub that, three-quarters of the time. At least he could get a break from her. She couldn't get away from her damn spiky self.

*Spiky. Bloody doctor.*

"So, you went, I take it?" he asked, pouring her another glass then one for himself — in a mug off the drainer, of all things. "I suggest going slower this time, drinking that — and no, I'm not being patronising, just caring. Plus, I don't want you throwing up. I have a new cream rug in the living room."

*What the hell?* "Are you *serious*? Talking to me about a sodding *rug* when you set me up with some doctor — if he really is one — who broke client confidentiality and started spouting bollocks at me about someone he's helped who *knows* me." Breaths coming out sharp and fast, Tracy steadied herself against the free-standing counter — island, whatever the hell it was called — and stared him directly in the eyes. "Did you even check him out before booking the appointment?"

"Yes."

"That's something then, but to top it off, it was that *weirdo* from the coffee shop. How *could* you?"

Damon had the grace to flush — as well he might. "I just . . . Listen, I wanted to help, and he dropped his cards. Actually, he swiped them off the table and —"

"You what? He *swiped* them? On *purpose*?" Christ, it made sense now. Dr Fuckface had recognised her in the coffee shop from the photo he'd seen, and he'd dropped those cards in the hope that . . . that what happened, happened. An appointment had been made, she'd attended, and there he had it, a new client to wind up. To fix. Or something.

"Now I think about it, yes, it could have been on purpose." Damon stroked his chin. His stubble rasped against his finger and thumb. "I just thought he was annoyed about something and flung the cards aside. You know, like when you throw your phone or a cup when things don't go your way."

Her mouth dropped open. "What is this? Pick on Tracy day?"

"I don't get what you're saying, love."

His eyes — they'd be her undoing if she gazed into them much longer.

"What I'm saying is, the doctor said some things that got under my skin, and now you're doing it." She sucked in a deep breath, the wine already doing a number on her, flowing through her veins, intent on sending her into a worse rage. She could allow it or . . . get herself under control. "It doesn't matter. Forget about it." Yes, she was taking the high road for once, although it rankled she'd done exactly what the doctor had predicted — taken it out on Damon. "I'm sorry. Shall I go outside, ring the bell, and start again?"

He smiled, relief bleeding into his features — the poor bastard. Was he always on tenterhooks around her? Were eggshells constantly under his feet? Did she make his life a living hell with the way she behaved? Why? Was she intent on sabotaging the only good thing that had happened to her?

*Seems so.*

"Really, I'm sorry. I'm a cow, I know that — and don't say I'm not. We both know I'm a nightmare. But I'm going to try, I promise, to watch my mouth and not let it run away with itself. It's going to be hard, because if what that doctor hinted at is true, someone — *him* — has been talking, and what gets me, is if he's admitted to what he's done, why hasn't the doctor told anyone?"

"You know why," Damon said. "He can't. It's confidential."

"It's not right. Just like priests knowing when people have killed someone or whatever. It isn't right."

"No, maybe it isn't, but why piss and moan about things you can't change? Why not focus on the things you *can*? Like pressing charges yourself." He sipped from his mug, then placed it on the worktop. Holding out his arms, he gave her another one of his lovely smiles. "Come here. You look like you need a hug."

She could be petulant and not go to him. She could leave him standing there, feeling foolish when she didn't walk into his embrace, but that wasn't the Tracy she was in this moment. Now — God, she'd been so many versions of herself since six o'clock — right now, she was the young girl before all of this had happened — or perhaps just after — when she needed a cuddle so badly it was a physical ache.

She stepped forward, and he wrapped his arms around her. She closed her eyes, cheek pressed to his chest, his heartbeat thudding beneath her ear, and let silent tears fall. He'd know she'd cried once she moved away — his shirt would be wet — but he wouldn't say anything, he never did these days. Not since she'd ripped him a new one for mentioning her tears a few months ago.

She was awful to him.

"I love you," she said. "And I mean I *love* you. Proper love. Not *that* love."

"I know. Shh now. We'll work this out. Will you go back? To the doctor, I mean?"

"You know I will. I'm not letting him get the better of me."

"I suspect he knows you'll be back, too."

"Probably. He wants to fix me? Good luck there, mate. I'll show him I can't be fixed. Smug bastard." She clutched him tighter, his scent like home, his warmth her safety net. "So, this rug. Can I roll around on it?"

"If that floats your boat."

"It does." She wiped her face, then stepped back, already missing his closeness. "Did you sign up for Netflix like you said you would?" She reached out for her wine. Took a small sip — to prove she could behave? Who knew. She didn't understand her actions any more than Damon did.

"I did. Want to watch something?" He grabbed the wine then led the way to the living room.

She sat on the sofa, her glass on the table beside it, and patted the seat next to her. The rug was gorgeous, and she stretched her legs out to dig her toes into the pile. "Pick something I don't have to concentrate on. It's been one hell of a day — and it'll only get worse from here on out until we catch this bastard."

Damon settled on the sofa and commandeered the remote. "Don't forget, it could be a woman."

"Do you really think so? The way she — if it is a she — has, for example, strung Mr Parks up . . . Honestly? Can you see it?"

"She could be built. You know, do weights and whatever. It's possible." Damon selected Netflix then browsed through the options.

Tracy, deflated and weak now all her anger had been spent, had the sense of her body sinking. Pleasant, as though she might fall asleep any second. Her phone buzzing put paid to that. She had no friends since her and Kathy had stopped spending time together, so it wouldn't be her trying to get hold of her, and it wasn't Damon, so . . .

"Ugh. You just know it's going to be work," Damon said. "Let's hope no one wants us to go back to the station. We've been drinking."

"One is fine." She tugged her phone from her pocket. Swiped the screen to answer. "Yes, boss."

"Busy, are you?" Chief Inspector John Aimes asked.

"Not particularly, though I really don't fancy working this evening."

"Hmm." John paused, then, "I could hand it over to the other team, but I think this is yours. Guts on display ring any bells, does it?"

"Dear God, another one? So soon?"

"My thoughts exactly. Are you on it?"

She sighed, the wine threatening to make a hasty exit. "Yes. Give me the details."

Damon had left the room and returned with a pad and pen. She took it, jotting down the information, then ended the call, wishing, not for the first time, she had a normal job with normal hours.

"Your toothbrush is in the usual place," Damon said.

Tracy rushed upstairs, brushed her teeth and tongue, and hoped that would be enough to disguise the smell of booze. Back in the hallway, she waited for Damon to get his coat, and they left the house, getting into her car. *How* long had this day been already?

With the engine rumbling, she eased out of her parking space and drove just a few streets away on the same estate. The thought of someone being killed while she'd raged at Damon took her on a guilt trip, the journey harsh and unforgiving.

Good. She deserved all the harshness life could give her.

Didn't she?

# CHAPTER ELEVEN

Covered head to toe in protective gear, Tracy stood on the path outside a terraced house, Damon beside her. PC Mitchum guarded the wooden gate, arms crossed over his chest. His flat hat slightly askew, he appeared as though he'd slapped it on quickly as he'd exited the police car, in a hurry to get to the victim.

"What have we got then, Mitchum?" Tracy asked, conscious of the body being ahead at the end of the path but not wanting to fully acknowledge it yet.

"Same as before, ma'am," Mitchum said. "He's been gutted."

"We must stop meeting like this," she quipped, rewarded with a shy smile from the officer. "Were you one of the first here?"

"Yes, ma'am."

"Farrell with you, was he?"

"Yes, ma'am. We were in the area so responded. Found him there." He jerked his head, indicating behind him. "Called it in, then secured the scene. Can't do anything about the gawkers, though. Sorry about that."

Tracy glanced around. Neighbours peered out of top-floor windows, lights off, probably so they could see better.

They resembled greyed-out ghouls, witnessing a train wreck without a train in sight. She'd bet no one had been at their window when the murder had taken place — again, she wasn't that lucky.

"Tent is on its way, I presume?" she asked.

"Yes, ma'am. ETA five minutes. Farrell's standing in front to shield the victim from being seen. Well, as much as he can do. Victim's wider than Farrell."

"Righty ho. Let's have a gander then, shall we, Hanks?" She turned to face Damon.

His grim expression said it all. He didn't want to view this body any more than he'd wanted to view Mr Parks. "Yes, ma'am." He swallowed, his Adam's apple quivering, the skin over it salted with goosebumps.

"Same rules apply as before; do you understand, Hanks?" Tracy didn't want to say anything outright in front of Mitchum.

Damon nodded, took in a huge breath.

*Poor bastard, but needs must.*

"Come on then." Tracy led the way, going through the gate then walking up the path to the front door. "Appreciate you standing here, Farrell. Very respectful." She gave a smile, a wonky one that didn't feel right; smiling with a deceased person a yard or so in front of you — unsettling, rude even.

"Thank you, ma'am." Farrell stepped aside, onto the grass beneath the window beside the door, hands clasped in front of him at his groin.

Damon sucked in a hissing breath between his teeth. His face paled, then spots of what resembled brown daubs in the darkness coloured his cheeks. Tracy initiated eye contact, willing him not to lose the plot. He nodded imperceptibly, and Tracy blew out a breath of relief. She nodded back. Faced the victim.

"Ah. I thought you'd caught your breath for another reason entirely. I see why you did that now. Mr Quinton, isn't it." There was no mistaking the pizza delivery man, wedged into the corner of the open porch, back half against the right-hand wall, the other half resting on the white UPVC door. Blood stained the door in a smeared, somewhat faint swath, where Mr Quinton had perhaps been sitting upright then had slid to one side. "What a bloody shame."

Tracy closed her eyes for a moment. Had the killer been watching, then? This was more than a coincidence. The odds of Quinton being the next victim — if the killings had so far been random — were slim. So maybe it *was* the woman he'd reported.

She opened her eyes to meet those of Quinton — wide, glassy, infused with fear. His mouth matched his neck — open and showing the contents, the mouth filled with gravestone teeth, the neck filled with fat globules, his windpipe just about visible, surrounded by flesh getting drier by the second.

"This is nasty," Damon said quietly. "She must have known he came to see us. She's been watching."

"We could suppose that, and if she hasn't, she'll know for sure tomorrow when the EFIT goes on the news. Maybe she'd have sought him out once she'd seen her likeness on TV. Maybe his days were numbered anyway."

She sighed, thinking of him rolling up his ciggies for the journey back after delivering a meal, of the lads who might miss him now he wouldn't be bringing their pizzas anymore. Of his wife — did he have one? Time would tell — his kids, his extended family. So many lives scarred by one person's need to sate some crazy urge that pushed them to kill. A ripple in a pond, one incident with far-reaching effects.

"I'll never understand people," she said. But she'd lied. She did understand. Understood the need to kill all too well. She'd imagined herself doing it too many times to count. Stabbing, suffocating — with a pillow or a plastic carrier bag, either would do — shooting — if she had a gun handy — or luring *him* to a train station or busy road and pushing his sorry arse in front of an express or HGV. Watching as the life bled out of him, taking his corrupt soul to Hell where he belonged.

"Me neither," Damon said, pulling her out of her heinous thoughts.

She switched back to her DI Collier self, leaving behind the version of Tracy she'd allowed to slip in. "Farrell, someone's called Kathy, right?"

"Yes, ma'am." He glanced at his watch. "Should be here any minute."

"Right. We'll wait. Hanks, ring in for a search on his address, please."

"Gladly." Damon walked away, to the gate, she presumed, or as far away from the body as he could get. At least he hadn't been sick this time.

Tracy thought about Quinton's position. It reminded her of the one time she'd tried to run from home. She'd been fifteen, desperate to get away, to find a better life, even if it meant living on the streets. A cardboard box as a roof would have been better than the slate tiles of home, a sleeping bag preferable to the scratchy blanket on her bed. Yet she hadn't been able to leave. She'd sat on the doorstep, back against the door, her toes, fingers, and the tip of her nose numb from the cold — her backside, too. She could have got up, walked off down the street and to the train station. She'd had fare money in her pocket, stolen from *his* wallet — she'd have been in London inside a couple of hours. But there she'd been, struck immobile on the doorstep, hands tucked into her sleeves for warmth.

The 'love' she'd endured had kept her rooted there, unable to find herself a place of safety. He'd opened the door sometime around four a.m., probably after going into her room for the very love she wanted to save herself from, and dragged her indoors, up the stairs, where he'd—

*Was* it possible these murders were linked to her? Each positioning brought memories splashing into her mind — all except the hanging until—

*'. . . You can go hang for all I care. Go on, get out, and don't ever come back.'*

*Oh God . . .*

"No," she whispered. "Please, no."

It couldn't be because of her, could it? He was warped — but *this* warped? Had her finally leaving got to him *that* much? Did he have it in him to orchestrate this kind of elaborate plan?

"Everything all right, ma'am?" Farrell came to stand beside her on the path, his paper booties *shhing* against the gravel.

"Err, yes. Thank you. I'll, um, just be out on the street."

Farrell returned to his place to shield Quinton, and Tracy, mind spinning, headed down the path, through the gate, and over to Damon, who stood in front of a hedge two houses down. The streetlight a few metres away cast an amber glow over his left side, his paper suit bringing on discombobulation, an out-of-body experience where she viewed him as something that didn't fit. A get-up like that never belonged on a residential street — never belonged anywhere. She wished the need for them didn't exist, that the world was full of goodness instead of evil.

"Did you get his address?" she asked, throwing off her unease and diving back into detective mode.

"Yes." Damon nodded. "Trace, I don't think I can—"

"Yes, you can." She gripped his wrist and squeezed. "We all feel like this at times. But we have to go on, have to do the next thing, which is going to see Quinton's family — assuming he has any." There was no way Quinton could be like the others and have no one — was there?

"A wife. Two adult kids." Damon sighed. "This is shit, d'you know that? All of it. The bad people, the need for folks like us doing the hard jobs, the deaths, the unfairness of life."

"Don't need to talk to me about unfairness." She could have cut out her tongue. There she was, bringing herself into the equation again when this was about Damon and his feelings. To cover up her selfishness, she said, "We've seen so much unfairness in our time as police officers. It comes with the territory. And this . . . this awful case we're dealing with . . . Isn't it better that it's us than some other team? We're dedicated, we want justice so much. Think of it that way. We care — more than we should at times, granted — but we get the job done. We're the best people for it, the best for those left behind."

"I know you're right, but—"

"Yes, I am — aren't I usually?" She smiled, hoping her words had taken the burden off his shoulders a little.

"How do you just bounce back all the time?"

"Case of having to." *Watch what you're saying — it's not about you, even though he's made it that way.* "We have to work with what we're given in this life and make the best of it." *Some people more than others, but hey, enough about me.* "Come on. We have a wife to visit. Kathy's here, look."

Damon sighed, a heavy one that seemed to come up from his toes. "Bloody hell . . ."

"Copper head on. Leave the civilian in you behind, understood?" She let go of his wrist. "Snap out of it, or do you want me to go all *ma'am* on you?"

He grinned at that — a small one, but a grin was a grin, and she'd take what she could get. Damon nodded, and together they walked towards Kathy, who stood talking to Mitchum at the gate.

*Don't let her make you change. Don't let her drag you back to your snarky behaviour.*

"Kathy, nice to see you again," she said, "although I wish it were under different circumstances."

"It's the only time I see you these days," Kathy sniped, curling her lip in an unbecoming sneer. "Can't remember the last time you had me on speed dial other than for picking my brains about the dead."

Kathy had once been a good friend, and Tracy thought back to when her phone had rung earlier, John on the other end telling her about the new murder. She'd known it would be work and not Kathy — because, really, they weren't friends anymore. Not like they used to be. And had they ever truly been friends? Tracy had never told her about *him* the whole time they'd been growing up.

"Ouch. Someone piss on your dinner?" Tracy bit back. "I would have said cornflakes, but given the time . . ."

"Oh, don't mind me. I'm just feeling lonely and abandoned. Thought I'd take it out on you. They say you lash out at the ones you love the most."

"Great that you love me, but lonely? You?" Tracy raised her eyebrows.

"Yes. The latest squeeze buggered off once he found out what I do for a living. He was good in the sack, too. Shame. This evening saw him scarpering mid-fumble."

"Why would you be talking about your job when being . . . fumbled?" Tracy frowned.

"Oh, I made a quip about cadavers. He didn't get the dark humour." Kathy shrugged, smiled, her eyes not joining in the joke. They held a sadness, a longing for something that had so far eluded her. Love — honest and true.

"I should think he didn't." Tracy patted Kathy's arm. "You need to date someone in your profession. What about that undertaker, Harry something-or-other?"

"Hmm." Kathy tapped her bottom lip. "Do you think there's a dating site for people like me? Graves R Us or something?"

"Christ, Kathy . . ." Despite the subject matter, Tracy laughed. "Right, back to work. We know the victim, so we're off to inform the wife. You take good care of him now." She tilted her head in Quinton's direction. "He's a good man. Was a good man."

"I'm not in the habit of treating the dead unfairly, Tracy, no matter who they are."

"I didn't mean that. Do you need a shag or something?"

"Or something, in my case. Vincent the Vibe will have to do the job now Fumbler is out of the picture."

Damon cleared his throat. Mitchum shuffled from foot to foot.

"Ah, I see I've said too much." Kathy turned towards two men walking down the pavement towards them. "Tent erection first, lads." She laughed at her own gag. "See you when I see you, Tracy, which will probably be over a morgue table rather than dining." She nipped behind Mitchum then up the gravel path.

*Sodding hell, she's pissed off with me.*

Tracy tugged Damon's arm and led the way to her car. Once inside, she faced Damon and asked, "How did I do that time?"

"You did well. Not cracking jokes at my expense is progress, but you were still a little terse. Jesus, she's a strange woman, don't you think?"

"I'm starting to see that, yes." Tracy sighed. "We were such good friends once. The job has changed her. Changed us all, I reckon."

Damon nodded. "Let's get this over with, then go back to mine. I'm feeling needy, like I want a cuddle. Tonight has got me out of sorts. Quinton, though . . . Fucking hell."

"I know."

*And if I told you what I suspected, you'd be on even more of a downer.*

She started the engine, letting the heater warm the interior for a few moments. Then she pulled away from the kerb, curious gawpers standing on the path craning their necks to watch her drive by. Who would *choose* to involve themselves in something like this, even if it *was* only observing?

She'd never understand that side of the public. After all, she hated seeing her own catastrophe of a life, let alone anyone else's. Why anyone would opt to observe trauma didn't bear thinking about.

*But you had a choice and you joined the force to do just that — deal with everyone's trauma. You choose to let images return inside your head. Again, you're judging; you're a hypocrite.*

*Leave me alone, will you? Just leave me alone.*

# CHAPTER TWELVE

Mrs Quinton had given a more appropriate response to the news than Mrs Parks. Julie Quinton had folded in on herself, her limbs loosening to the point she'd collapsed in front of her sofa, smacking her head on the hardwood floor, going out for the count for a few seconds then coming round, groggy and clearly confused as to why Tracy and Damon were crouched beside her. Then realisation had crept up on her, and Tracy had stared in wonder as the light of recollection flared bright and horrid in the woman's eyes — the knowledge that this wasn't a dream, that her husband had been murdered, and she'd have the children to tell, his mother — oh, his poor, poor mother; Maureen didn't deserve that, not so soon after losing her own husband. On and on it had gone, Julie babbling, Damon holding her tight as she'd sobbed so hard Tracy had worried the distraught woman would fall apart.

That part of the job threatened to break Tracy every time, but she always remained strong, one step removed, almost as though she stood on the outside looking in, a part of it but not, there but far in the distance, where nothing could hurt her.

Tracy shifted her thoughts elsewhere, away from the harrowing experience at the Quinton house, the latest crime scene, her visit to Dr Fuckface — had that really been only a few hours ago? It seemed a lifetime had passed since she'd stormed out of there, vulnerable and off-kilter. Afraid, too — yes, afraid the Past was coming back to get her once and for all this time, dragging her backwards when she so desperately wanted to move forwards, to the white picket fence, the husband, the dog, and maybe a tropical fish tank.

"This is so good," she said, glancing up and across at Damon. She pointed her fork at the pasta he'd cooked once they'd arrived at his place. Dining at the table — they didn't do enough of that, usually grabbing meals on the go and eating them in the car or at the roadside, rain soaking them or the sun baking them. "This sauce — the cream will go to my hips, but what the hell. Can't remember the last time you cooked for me."

"Or you cooked for *me*." He smiled, a sad one, the type she didn't care for. "It'll always be like this, won't it? Eating at crazy-fuck-o'clock, our time together interrupted by death or some other crime. By bastards who have no respect for the law, who think it's their divine right to kill people, maim, hurt — so much hurt."

"This isn't like you, love," she said, resting her fork against her plate and reaching out to grasp his free hand.

"What isn't?" He speared a piece of cream-sauce-covered fusilli and twisted his fork so the food rotated.

"You being negative. It's usually the other way around. I'm the Debbie Downer in this relationship, not you. Taking my crown, are you? Rude . . ."

He shrugged. Didn't smile. Stared down at his dinner as if the plate held worms not pasta. "I don't know. This . . . All this . . ." He took his hand from beneath hers and thumped his chest. "Too much on the old ticker. Maybe I'm just tired."

"Maybe."

They finished eating in silence, and after clearing up and loading the dishwasher, they settled in bed — Damon without clothes, Tracy fully dressed; he didn't question that

— and she gave him the cuddle he'd asked for earlier, until he fell asleep. She hoped he didn't dream, or at least if he did, it was a happy one.

Wired, her mind too full of information she couldn't piece together into a coherent solution yet, Tracy eased away, careful not to wake him. She crept downstairs, where she slipped on her footwear then grabbed her phone off the coffee table in the living room, sliding it into her pocket.

Outside, the air gave her a bit of a slap, and she walked to her car to take out her coat. Once on, it didn't chase away the chill as she'd hoped, only giving slight respite from the biting wind that chose to gnaw at the tops of her ears with pin-sharp teeth and slither down the back of her neck, sneaking beneath her top. She shivered, zipped up, then, in her car, she headed towards home.

But not the one she lived in now. *That* home.

*What am I doing?*

She had no idea, but she parked two houses down from the home where she'd grown up. That front door — again she remembered how she'd sat there that 'runaway' night, frozen in more ways than one.

*He* still lived there. She hadn't let access to the database go unused. She'd tracked the fucker since the day she'd joined the force, and for the umpteenth time, she wondered why she'd stuck around here. Why she still lived in a city where she could bump into him at any moment. Odd that she hadn't fled for a safer haven. Odd she hadn't set eyes on him since her mother's funeral, too, or the time before that when she'd walked out of that house, him undoubtedly calling her a bitch, but she hadn't heard it because she'd slammed the front door, blocking out the sound of him, the sight of him.

Shame that slam hadn't erased him for good. She heard and saw him in her head most days — he'd taunt her until her dying day. He was on her skin, in her scars. The lumpy, burnt skin on her legs *was* him — him underneath the puckered surface, trying to get out, wanting to remind her he'd always be with her no matter what she did.

Moving in with Kathy after leaving had been her only option. Kathy had been well on her way to becoming an pathologist, studying like crazy every moment she'd got. Whereas Tracy — what had she had? Minimal money, what with being on the social at the time, average GCSE results, and a whole fucked-up life behind her. It had taken ages to get into the police force — she'd failed twice before finally being accepted. Her confidence had soared from rock-bottom to cloud nine the day she'd been informed of her success. She'd left the waitress job she'd slaved away at, having found the position three months after she'd invaded Kathy's home; two years she'd slogged there, praying *he* didn't turn up for a bacon butty and a cup of coffee so strong he could 'stand his spoon up in it'. And, with her new job, she'd vowed to show him, to put the damn wind up him that *she* had the power now — she could haul his arse in any time she wanted.

So why hadn't she?

All those lies — that was the problem. She'd covered for him for years, allowed him to carry on with someone else now she wasn't there. She conveniently, selfishly, didn't think about that side of things too much — self-preservation had a habit of ensuring you cared for number one, and not number two, three, four or more. She'd paid a heavy price, and her purse was now empty, no more coins or notes to give anyone else in his life.

She'd convinced herself he'd stopped. He wouldn't want to risk her catching him in the act with a new one, not now she was a copper. Then again, maybe he'd bargained on exactly what she was doing now — hiding from the fact she'd allowed him to do what he had, not wanting anyone to know she'd craved his 'love' as much as she'd despised it.

How could she tell anyone that when she'd curled up on Kathy's lumpy sofa each night, the shaft of orange from the streetlight burgling the living room through the crack in the curtain — how could she tell anyone she'd *missed* his 'love'?

That wasn't right, wasn't normal, but miss it she had.

She was just as warped as him.

She shook herself into the present, a shiver pillaging her body despite the heater going full pelt. Refocussing, her vision somewhat blurry until she concentrated to clear it, she contemplated that house and what it meant to her now. It was a prison, a keeper of secrets, its walls bulging with the sights they'd witnessed — terrible sights, terrible sounds, wailing, pleading, crying.

Grunts.

*Fuck off.*

The front door was exactly the same, albeit weathered from years of rain, cold winter temperatures, and blazing summer sun, which always hit it bang on noon; her bedroom, front-facing, had become an oven. Hell during summer nights when his skin had touched hers.

"Stop it, Collier, you morbid bitch," she muttered.

A light burnt in her old bedroom window, and she wondered what he used the room for, seeing as Mum was dead, off with the angels — or with the Devil himself, atoning for her sins, for her part in the lies.

The curtains, although closed, twitched. Someone brushing them as they walked by? Then they parted in the middle, just a tad, and a centre slice of a figure stood there. She imagined *him* staring out, at her illuminated by the interior light in the car — shit, why had she switched it on; had she wanted him to see her? Did she *want* him to know she'd come back, giving him the idea he still had control over her?

That was all it took to start the car and think about driving away. Except the curtains parted fully, and the sliver became a full person. It might have been the distance playing tricks on her, but she'd swear her mother stood there, but with a different hairstyle. None of the short, bouncy curls from hair wrapped around rollers overnight — no, this mother had long hair, straight, as far as Tracy could tell. She inched out of the parking spot to slowly ease forward until she idled the car directly outside the house.

Dangerous, that.

The woman didn't move — it wasn't her mother, couldn't possibly be — and just gazed out, making eye contact, a smirk on her lips. Lips the same as Tracy's, if a little fuller. This person, she looked like Tracy imagined her mother had when she'd been younger, before her children had come along, when she'd first met the monster who would defile those children as if they were his property.

Tracy blinked once, twice, and the figure was gone, the light out, curtains shut, as though whoever it had been hadn't stood there at all.

*I'm imagining things now?*

Yes, she was. The mind played tricks on you, especially when you had trauma to deal with, and she had it in spades. She'd studied all about PTSD, knew the signs — Jesus, she had them herself. Maybe she ought to tell Dr Fuckface about them. Let him dig about inside her head and dish out some pills for her trouble. Send her away with a prescription that would do nothing but mess her up even more.

*No. No drugs.*

But she had to do something. She begrudgingly admitted, while driving out of that damned street, that Damon had been spot on; he'd done the right thing in making that appointment. She couldn't go on like this, seeing things that weren't there. Seeing people who no longer existed, in a body that wasn't theirs.

It was time to face the Past and all the terrible things in it.

Time to be the Tracy Damon deserved.

Maybe the Tracy *she* deserved, too.

# CHAPTER THIRTEEN

He's not happy. Says I've messed up. I want to shrug, to tell him to go and do one, but I don't have the guts.

Guts.

Messy things, they are.

It's cold in here. He's stingy about the heating. Says we should wrap up in layers rather than toast ourselves silly with artificial heating. I should be used to it, but during the times I'm on the hunt and I go into shops, the warmth is a hug I've craved for years, comforting, special, needed.

I try to persuade him to let me out again tomorrow, to reach his goal of ten sooner, but he isn't having any of it. Says I've done the deed too close to home tonight, and coppers might come calling, their enquiries including us. After all, we live one street away from where Pizza Man delivered his last meal.

Seems I'll only ever please *him* when he shows me love.

"Oh, it's all right for you," he says, "hidden away as you are, but I'd have to talk to them, and that isn't ideal."

I can see his point. If the police call and ask to come in, what if they do a search of the house and find the knife? Find me? I point that out to him, and he says that won't happen

— they have to have a warrant, probable cause, whatever the eff they are.

I wouldn't know about such things.

Like he'd said to me once: You know nothing, Jon Snow.

What the hell that meant, I don't know. I'm not called Jon.

He'd laughed, the sound a gurgle, and went on about dragon eggs and their mother, some blonde woman who doesn't get burnt by fire, unlike *some* people.

I think he's getting more deranged as the years go by.

*Join the club.*

He dismisses me, and I go to a room I'm not meant to go to. No more than five minutes pass, and I jump from a knock at the door. It's a rap of authority, scary, like the one the courier uses when he delivers *his* 'love tools' from Amazon.

I hope the person at the door hasn't brought more tools. The last one . . . hurt.

Panic takes hold, wringing my stomach with a fierce, unyielding grip. I'm not meant to be in this part of the house — stupid of me to have come here — but I can't get into the basement without whoever it is at the front door seeing me. *He's* going to go mad when he finds out where I am. Maybe if I wait for him to go to sleep, then creep into my room . . .

"Good evening, sir." Whoever that is, his voice is muffled, like *he* hasn't opened the door fully. "We're doing house-to-house enquiries — sorry to trouble you so late, but there's been an incident in Primrose Road, and we wondered if you'd noticed anything suspicious in the last few hours."

"Suspicious?" he says — he's good at sounding surprised. Good at sounding everything, chameleon that he is.

My stomach churns; I don't feel very well.

"I'm afraid I've been in all night with the curtains closed," he goes on. "Haven't heard or seen a thing."

"Your wife, then? Or another family member?"

"My wife is dead, and I live alone."

"Sorry to hear that, sir. Thank you for your time."

The front door closes so quietly, I'm convinced I imagine the soft snick as the latch meets its keeper.

Funny, I'm a latch, and he's my keeper.

He's got me locked up tight, even though I'm allowed outside the house to complete his requests, allowed, over the years, to get some shopping in. Even out there I'm jailed, by my emotions, my fear, by his threats.

I tried to get away once. Told him I'd tell Mum what he was doing if he didn't let me go. When Mum had gone to stay in a hotel for a week after he'd punched her face, her eye as black as the coal in the shed out the back, he'd tied me up in that same shed and soundproofed the basement, had a steel-backed door fitted, the side that faced the hallway wooden, so no one would wonder why a metal one was there. So Mum wouldn't wonder.

My new room was the basement. I asked once where Mum thought I was, and he'd said, "You ran away, you ungrateful bitch, and she's up there crying for the loss of you. Think on that next time you get it in your head to leave me. Think of how upset your actions make people."

I'd dwelt on that for years, about how selfish I'd been to want to leave. I reminded myself he loved me, that what he did was special — not all fathers could bring themselves to love their child in that way; that's what he'd said anyway.

I wait now — I'm a pro at that, marking time — until he climbs the stairs, walking across the landing with its ominous creak outside one particular bedroom door. It seems he pauses, and I wonder if he's thinking of the past and how it used to be.

# CHAPTER FOURTEEN

An eerie, younger version of her mother gazed back at Tracy from the printout of the image the artist had cobbled together with various face parts, then merged them on his computer to create a flawless photograph that appeared real, a snapshot, a mugshot even. No dark curly hair, though — it hung straight, the same as the apparition at her old bedroom window. A chill ran down her spine — her mind playing tricks on her once more — and she batted her eyelashes to dissolve the vision.

It remained the same.

There was a plausible explanation for this. People had similar features; people could resemble one another. This woman was no different to others she'd sworn were someone else when they hadn't been. Mistaken identity was as common as smartphones. And why had Mr Quinton described her as a girl? This was a woman — her crows' feet gave her age away, as did the fine lines crawling out of her top lip to stretch towards her nose — but maybe Quinton had seen her as younger because he'd been closing in on his sixties before he'd died.

Age perception could be so off it was laughable. Years of taking witness statements had shown her that. How many times had three people described the same person, each account different? In one case, the person had been overweight, slim, average-sized, with blonde, brown, or ginger hair, their tattoo a dragon, a rose, or a face. When the criminal had been apprehended, they'd had black hair, were underweight, and had no ink on them whatsoever.

Happy with her reasoning, she placed the EFIT on Roger's stack of files, sat on his desk, shrugged, and waited for the news to start. Her men stood in front of the flat-screen TV on the wall beside the white board, an advert blarting on about the latest shampoo that was infused with caffeine — like hair could get a boost from it. People fell for any gimmick if it was marketed the right way.

A bit like she had with *him* — until she'd woken up.

It dawned on her that life was full of lies — everywhere you looked, there was an untruth. Hardly anything did what it said on the tin.

The opening credits of the local morning news filled the screen, the serious music abrading her nerves. Tracy held her breath, hoping their case was the first story so they could get on with their day instead of biting their nails for their segment to come on. Of course, Mark, Stuart, and Roger would be stuck inside fielding calls from the public after the appeal, as well as doing their usual tasks. As for Tracy and Damon — Tracy had Forensics to badger for results, maybe a visit to see Mr Quinton in the morgue, and Damon, well, he'd be better off doing paperwork, the mood he was in.

"Good morning. Police are requesting the public's help in identifying a person of interest in recently committed crimes," the newscaster said.

*Good, she hasn't mentioned the specific offences.*

"A woman is wanted for questioning in connection with a spate of murders carried out in the last few days . . ."

*Fuck!*

". . . anyone who thinks they recognise this woman should contact . . ."

Tracy switched the TV off. "*How* many times did I stress the crime shouldn't be broadcast? Bloody hell. Don't they realise the outcry there's going to be because we haven't alerted the public as to what's been going on before now?" She thumped Stuart's desk with the side of her fist, incensed at how the media didn't give a monkeys about the fallout from reporting something like that. "Next time, I'll do the appeal myself. At least then I'm in control of outgoing information." She gripped her hair, tugging with both hands, aware she'd slipped into one of her old selves.

The men stared at her.

Only Damon had ever seen this side of her. He looked at her; he wanted to walk over to her and hug it all away, his expression told her that, but she let her hair go, shaking her head slightly — *no, don't come near me, not in front of the others.*

"It might be to our advantage, boss," Mark said, sitting behind his desk and accessing some file or other on his computer, his back to her.

She tamped down her anger so she didn't blast him with the vitriol swirling just below the surface. "How so?" She threaded her fingers through her hair to smooth it.

He swivelled his chair to face her. It squeaked, the sound jarring. "If people know it's murder, they'll be more inclined to give us information through fear — they'll want her caught. If they think she's just robbed a convenience store a few times or whatever, what will they care? She's not a threat to them just by shoplifting or demanding money from the till. But killing people . . . See what I mean?"

Thank goodness for the rational thinking of her team member — all of them, actually, tended to calm her when she went off the rails.

"You're right, of course. Sorry." She let out a long breath, and it took away some of the weight she'd been lugging around since this case had begun. "I'm just so frustrated. We followed Mr Quinton for days without any need, and while doing that, someone else has been bumping people off. We didn't even twig it couldn't be him because we'd been following him most nights and would have known what he was up to. Scrambled minds, the lot of us. Which reminds me — have you all sorted time off yet?"

All four shook their heads.

"Do it now — go on, off with you. No more work until you've booked a break. You can't keep going like this, and neither can I. We're making stupid mistakes, and the chief is going to rip my girl balls off when he finds out — unless we can give him an update that means we have a lead on who this woman is. Get on with it — *before* the phones go crazy."

She left the room. In her office, she closed the door and leant against it, sinking to the floor and hugging her knees. Again, she remembered the 'runaway' time. Why did simple gestures that mirrored the Past always trigger memories she didn't want to entertain? Why did she associate *everything* with what had gone before? If she kept doing it, eventually, all she'd think about was the Past and nothing else. And she'd been so good up until now, successfully stowing it all away, living a life based on lies but appearing as a 'normal' individual. For the most part.

Should she pay *him* a visit and let him know she had her eye on him?

Not likely. That would be doing what her team had suggested regarding Mr Quinton when he'd been a suspect. She'd shot them down as if they were stupid, and hark at her now, thinking of doing the same thing. It was always the same with her: Do as I say, not as I do.

No, he'd know they were on to him and change his behaviour. Best she wait. And when should she tell the team what she suspected? It was her job to give full disclosure — she shouldn't be withholding information from her men or the chief.

Did she care that much about her part in the lies that she was willing to let *him* carry on killing people?

*But the suspect is a woman, not a man.*

So who the hell *was* the woman? What was she to him? Or was Tracy's mind putting two and two together and coming up with a number so high it was ridiculous? Did she want him to be behind this so badly that she'd waste more precious time — her team's time, the taxpayers' money — chasing a spectre that hadn't done anything but expect her to love him, screwing her up in the process?

She studied herself from an outsider's perspective. A DI at thirty-two — and she'd worked damn hard to get there, too, no shagging the higher-ups, just pure detective work and a passion to put bad people behind bars. A woman who appeared to have it all together, well-balanced, knowing where she wanted to go and determined on getting there.

The reality was totally the opposite. She wore a mask — several of them depending on the situation, something to hide behind so no one saw the real Tracy, the stupid little cow who—

Since the first murder, she'd been unsettled, ill at ease in her own skin, like it didn't belong to her anymore. Like she lived inside another person who had allowed her mind to conjure scenarios that were based on fiction, not fact.

*Him* orchestrating the murders?

*Come on now. You don't believe that, do you?*

She staggered to her feet, her body and mind lethargic. She wanted nothing more than to go home, climb under the duvet, and sleep this crap away.

At her desk, she slid an A4 pad in front of her and jotted down the information so far:

> VICTIM #1: MICHAEL ROBBINS, 35, GUTTED, POSED IN HIS HOME IN FRONT OF A THREE-BAR FIRE.
>
> VICTIM #2: LEE TRIPPER, 32, GUTTED, POSED IN HIS HOME INSIDE A WARDROBE, A KNITTED, RAINBOW-STRIPED SCARF TIED AROUND HIS HEAD, COVERING HIS EYES.
>
> VICTIM #3: URWIN PARKS, 38, GUTTED, POSED HANGING.

VICTIM #4: WILLIAM QUINTON, 59, GUTTED, POSED AGAINST A FRONT DOOR.

Her mind zipped back *there* again. She tried to stop it, but the images stubbornly elbowed their way into her head, a tumble of visuals she'd watched so many times before — and had once lived.

It wasn't her imagination. Those poses — she'd been in every one of them at some point while under his roof. They were too specific to be a coincidence. All right, the hanging related to what he'd said rather than her actually hanging, but still.

She ripped the page from the pad, folded it, then slid it into her jacket pocket. Instead of snagging on her mobile, which she'd taken to putting in her trouser pocket since that morning, it caught on something else.

Dr Fuckface's business card.

Eyeing the desk phone, she debated on whether to call him. Was she ready to see him so soon after her major flounce yesterday? Was he ready to see *her*, assuming he had any slots available today?

She drew the card out of her pocket, annoyed the folded paper came out with it, dropping to the desk. She jabbed in his number.

"Good morning, Schumer and Schumer, Angel speaking. How may I help you?"

Schumer *and* Schumer?

"Hi, it's Tracy Collier. I was wondering if any appointments were available today."

"Oh, it's you."

*What?* "Ex*cuse* me?"

"I'm sorry. Pardon me. Is it an emergency?"

"Define emergency."

"Do you have thoughts of suicide, self-harm, hurting others, delusions, hallucinations—"

"Yes, yes."

"Which one?"

Pause. "All of them except committing suicide."

"Oh dear, you are a one, aren't you?"

Was that a *titter* coming through the line?

"Is there anyone else I can speak to apart from you?" Tracy snapped.

"No, just me or Dr Schumer."

"So he's the boss? The person I make a complaint to?" Tracy seethed, trying her hardest to remain polite.

"*We're* the boss. What would you like to complain about?"

"I hardly think it's conductive to complain to you *about* you, Angel. Your telephone manner leaves a lot to be desired. I'm surprised Dr Schumer has any clients at all if you treat them the way you've treated me."

"Oh, no, I don't treat everyone this way — just those Dr Schumer obsesses over."

Alarm bells jangled inside Tracy's head. She shouldn't go to see him again, but something in her urged her on. He knew things she wanted to know. He might be able to fix her. And if Angel wanted to be rude every time, Tracy could handle that.

"Is that wise, Angel?" she asked.

"Probably not, but when your husband has affairs with clients, and you sit there in reception hearing certain things, it wears a little thin."

"He's your *husband*?" Tracy's mouth dropped open. She snapped it shut. It wasn't often she was dumbfounded, but . . .

"Yes. And?" Angel was too sarcastic for words.

"I assure you, I'm happy in my current relationship. No offence, but Dr Fu — Schumer doesn't do it for me. I see him as a therapist and nothing else."

"Oh, but he's so much more," she whispered. "Be careful."

Heart thumping hard, Tracy whispered back, "What do you mean?"

"I've said too much. Your appointment is at two for an hour and a half. Goodbye."

Tracy lowered the phone from her ear and widened her eyes at it. What the hell had just gone on there? Angel was a snarky woman, no doubt about it, but was it any surprise if what she'd said was true? And as for warning Tracy to be careful . . . She was a police officer — no one could mess with her now.

If they did, they'd better be prepared to die trying.

# CHAPTER FIFTEEN

"You do realise I can't shit wonders and piss miracles, don't you, Tracy?" Kathy studied her, pages of reports held at chest height, her eyes wide and glaring.

*She'll have an aneurism in a minute if she isn't careful.*

Tracy was about to say as much but stopped herself. Didn't seem the dark joke would wash with her colleague today.

*Colleague. Is that how I see her now?*

"God," she said, "I only asked if you had anything on Mr Parks yet. If I'd wanted to know about Mr Quinton, *then* you might be able to chew my arse."

Kathy blushed, bright red spots on her prominent cheekbones, purple on the outside, reminding Tracy of a corona around the sun. Something had chapped Kathy's nipples, and it wouldn't be long before she said what it was if she stayed true to form.

"Why are you even bothering me in person?" Kathy asked. "A phone call would've been enough. You don't usually come down here, where the stink of death gets in your precious hair." She flung the papers onto her desk. A few left the sheaf and flew up, then gracefully fluttered to the floor, landing in a random pattern, inches apart. "Great, now I'm going to have to put them in order again. Thanks for that."

"What? Not my fault. Something you need to get off your chest, is there? Or is it the fact you want something *on* your chest — namely a man's mouth — that has you so worked up?"

Kathy threw her head back and laughed — hard — but Tracy doubted it was because she'd said something funny. This was a reaction hiding a deeper problem. Tracy would give her five minutes to spit it out, and if she didn't, Kathy could wallow in her own shit.

"I'm 'worked up', as you put it, because I'm overburdened and underpaid, I have no boyfriend — *again* — there are bills to pay, the car's broken down — apparently needs a new carburettor or some bollocks like that — and I've put on eighteen pounds. My favourite red dress no longer fits me; I'm spilling out of the damn thing, for Pete's sake. Do I need to go on?"

Tracy frowned. It had only been recently Kathy had a bee in her bonnet, so had her life gone downhill in the last few days?

"I'd say I'd give you a shoulder to cry on, but I need one myself." Tracy had done it again — brought herself into the equation when someone else had a problem, switching it around so it became all about her. She had to get out of that habit. It was a bastard thing to do.

Kathy dropped to her knees to pick up the fallen papers. "You, Miss Got-It-Together, needs a shoulder to cry on? Since when has that happened? When did your halo go skew-whiff, Perfect Penny?"

Kathy's passive-aggressive jibes were wearing thin. She was a perfect candidate for Facebook, slinging up memes that said one thing but meant another.

Tracy sighed. "You know me, I grin and bear it. But this time, these murders . . . Something isn't right."

"See, that's part of the problem. You have these hunches, and they take over, blinding you to everything else — to everyone else. You focus on the hunch, like you did with Mr Quinton — yes, ouch, I noticed, let's hope the chief doesn't — and sometimes you mess up. Cut yourself some slack, will you?"

"Cutting slack is bullshit, Kathy. That doesn't get things done. Forgiving myself for messing up doesn't get things done." The real meaning behind those words hit Tracy with blunt force. If she forgave herself for the Past, her drive to be a copper wouldn't be there anymore. Would it?

"You need a break, like me," Kathy said. "You don't seem to have time for anyone these days, do you? It's work and Damon, Damon and work, sod everyone and everything else."

And there it was, Kathy's issue, out in the open and morphing into a huge elephant that stood in the corner, ogling them. Tracy acknowledged it, resisted giving it the finger, and attempted to smile at Kathy. She failed, a pout twisting her lips instead.

"Right, so, you're saying what you're *really* pissed off about isn't your life hitting a rough patch, but me seeing Damon, is that it? Christ, Kathy, *how* old are you? Are we still back in school? Did I miss the memo that we weren't really adults who have our own lives to lead, which means we might not have as much time for one another like we used to? I'm sorry we don't meet up at the pub every week anymore, if that's your beef, but if you worked as much as me, all you'd want to do in the evening is go home and go to bed."

Kathy stood and slapped the papers on her desk.

Tracy shook her head, sad it had come to this. "Fine. If that's the way you want it. If you don't have any information for me regarding Mr Parks or Mr Quinton yet, I'll be off. Once you *do* have information, please email it to me. When you've climbed down from that super-high horse you're galloping on, let me know. I'll find some time to massage your swollen ego. Oh, and a ride is *definitely* what you need. Victor isn't doing a good enough job, obviously. Join that dating site you were going on about. Only another cadaver carer could put up with you."

*Miaow, but sodding hell . . .*

Tracy left Kathy's office, walking along the corridor, trying not to breathe. The scent of death mixed with cleaning products made for a disgusting smell. She understood Kathy's upset, but Tracy had so much on her plate at the moment, in her head, in her life — things Kathy couldn't even begin to understand — that she had no desire to talk things out with the woman and explain why she'd retreated into her shell and only wanted to be with Damon outside of work.

Her lungs burnt through lack of air, so she sipped a little, hoping it could carry her to the exit without her body needing more.

Maybe Tracy should have confessed her life to Kathy way back when — then she'd be more tolerant of Tracy's decision to concentrate on her relationship with Damon instead of the one with Kathy. But now Tracy was glad she'd stuck by her decision not to — nice as Kathy had been to her up until a few seconds ago, she was a gossip, and *that* kind of information was dangerous in her hands.

If Kathy couldn't handle Tracy's lack of spare time and her relationship with Damon, she needed to get a damn life — and another friend who could handle her caustic comments and schoolgirl drama.

Annoyed that Kathy had yet again reduced her to a snarky bitch, what with Tracy's last few comments to her, she shoved open the glass door and breezed out, her face heating, and berated herself for so easily falling back into Kathy's way of acting. Tracy should have more control over herself — it wasn't all Kathy's fault.

*That's big of you . . .*

*Leave off, it's step in the right direction, taking some of the blame.*

Out in the car park, she took a moment to sit in her car without any distractions. She still had forty minutes on her ticket. There was always something going on these days — emails to answer, telephone calls to take, bodies to visit, her team to lead. No wonder she was overwhelmed and experiencing the sensation of being out of her depth. It should be an old friend, that feeling, but she hated it with a passion and wished she could just—

Had she been about to utter the first emergency in Angel's list?

*'Do you have thoughts of suicide . . .'*

No. Never. She'd never let *him* win to that degree.

She started the car, slammed it into gear, and drove off, attempting to enter that place in her head where nothing existed. It was a struggle to get in there — malicious forces seemed to want to keep her out — but she managed it, finding a measure of peace, solace that had been sorely missing lately.

She drove a few miles then pulled over into a lay-by, calling Damon to let him know where she was going next.

"You're going back to the doctor so soon?" he asked.

God, it was good to hear his voice.

"Yes. I've got some things on my mind — I need to talk about them to someone not involved with the case."

"Is it wise to do that with him? I mean, look at how he told you things he shouldn't have before. He's hardly stuck to the handbook on confidentiality, has he."

"No, you're right."

"Seriously? I'm right? Wonders will never cease."

She smiled at that, giggled, pleased he sounded more like his old self. It was one thing for her to be unhappy, but she no longer wanted to be the cause of making *him* unhappy. She had some growing up to do, and it started now. "Okay, I'll see how it goes. Me talking about my past shouldn't be news to him if *he's* told him everything already."

"He might not have. Not all of it."

"True. Anyway, my appointment is at two for an hour and a half, so if John asks, I'm out somewhere making enquiries, I didn't tell you where."

"Trace . . . I've told you before about involving me in things like this. I don't want to lose my job if I get caught covering for you."

"Sorry, won't do it again. This is the last time, promise."

He sighed. "All right."

Guilt rippled inside her because he'd relented again — anything for her, he'd once said. She took advantage of that and had to pack it in. "Anyway, if it makes you feel better, me going to see Schumer might have everything to do with the case."

"I don't understand."

She imagined his frown and smiled again, wishing he sat beside her, his hand on her thigh. "No, you're not meant to. Not until I'm sure I'm right."

"I hate it when you're cryptic."

"Better than me being salty."

"You're not wrong there. Oh, before you go, and talking of cryptic, a strange phone call came in after you'd left earlier regarding the suspect. Some old lady said she recognised her, only the EFIT was of a woman she used to know years ago. I wanted to tell you this in person, but . . . You said your mum's name was Paula, right?"

"Yes . . ." *Where the hell is this going?*

"Well, the old dear said the EFIT was of Paula Collier. Now, I know this can't be true because your mum's dead, so—"

"Got to go." Tracy ended the call, her stomach churning. Bile promised to visit her mouth. The welcome mat wasn't out for it, and she inhaled through her nose, hoping her head would stop spinning. It didn't, so she rested her brow on the steering wheel, nauseated and wondering if she could manage to drive to the therapist's place after all.

Paula Collier? The old lady had to be wrong. Tracy's mother had died — and she'd been much older than the woman in the EFIT when she had. Tracy had attended the funeral — well, she'd hidden behind a huge oak so she didn't have to be near *him*. She'd cried as the coffin lowered into the ground, sniffles and quiet sobs stabbing at the cold air, roses flung from many different people — and who were they anyway? Her mother hadn't had any friends as far as Tracy knew.

This could mean the case could go in a direction she wasn't ready for it to go in yet. She needed it to be on her terms, but fate had shown her ugly face and butted her nosy beak into Tracy's business.

She wished she hadn't cut Damon short. She should have asked if only *he* knew about the call. If so, he could have followed it up himself and kept the others on the team in the dark. But that would be her, yet again, expecting him to be underhand on her behalf, and hadn't she just promised him she wouldn't do that anymore?

*Shit.*

Calmer now, anger fuelling her instead of confusion, she continued her journey, intent on seeing Dr F. and playing the therapist herself, getting information out of *him* instead of the other way around.

# CHAPTER SIXTEEN

He's like a bulldog chewing a wasp today — an angry, stung bastard, all thunder and lightning, a storm blowing mean gusts of wind my way. I don't like it, but it's not as if I can do anything about it, is it? He holds all the cards until we reach number ten, so I'm better off shutting my mouth and getting on with it.

The basement is colder than usual, which is odd, because with the amount of heat coming off him, it should be roasting. He'll lose steam eventually, he always does, and then I can make him feel better with love.

He's pacing, back and forth, back and forth, his face frozen in that angry grimace he has when something's got his back up. It's me, I know that — he's said so enough, so I'm not likely to have got the wrong end of the stick.

"That policeman calling last night," he says. "Didn't I *tell* you that would happen?"

"Yes."

"Didn't I *say* they'd do house-to-bloody-house?"

"Yes."

"Next time, do *not* stop walking until you're *at least* two miles from here, like the first three. Why did you choose Number Four? Why?"

I'm not sure whether to admit Pizza Man saw me those two times. *He* might go off on one, hitting me like he did once when I wet the bed out of fear. It was ages ago, when I didn't understand love was love, and I'd tried to push him off me, crying, begging him to leave me alone, but he wouldn't, wouldn't . . .

"He was just there," I say. "Easy target. You said to pick the easiest ones."

"Yes, but not around here. Christ . . ." He sifts his hand through his thinning grey hair, his fingers thick, stubby sausages, red and chapped from all that work he does in the allotment, even though it's bitter cold out. His skin rasps whenever he touches mine.

Why doesn't he shave that comb-over off? He reminds me of that murderer from the olden days, with his circular, wire-rimmed specs and shiny scalp. Can't think of his name. Crispin or something. Creepy sod, anyway.

"You've gone inside your head," he says. "Stop doing that. You know I dislike it when you stare and rock."

"Sorry." I am, too. I should do as I'm told, act normal so he'll set me free like he promised. "I didn't mean to."

"No, you never do."

"Will the police be back?" I ask.

"You'd better hope not, for your sake."

That didn't sound good.

He blusters on, but I'm not listening. I think about freedom and living in a place of my own where I can have the heating on instead of mountains of clothes. I'll eat *all* the things — look at my full plate of cakes, *look at them* — and not have to worry about giving love when I don't want to.

Will I miss him? I'm sure I will. He's been there for me, my captor, my bully, my saviour, my abuser, the one constant that hasn't wavered. I owe him for putting up with me, for having me here when he could have anyone he wanted, so he's said. I feel guilty sometimes for holding him back — he said that, too — but now he's going to let me fly . . . once I find six others and finish the job.

". . . so, repeat what I just said. I need to know you're aware of exactly what you must do." He stops pacing and walks over to stand in front of my bed — it's a mattress on the floor, but still a bed.

Oh. I have no idea what he's been saying. "Tell me again, just so I'm sure, then I'll repeat it."

He frowns, canting his head to one side, and glares at me with those god-awful eyes of his. "Right. So this is what you'll do . . ."

# CHAPTER SEVENTEEN

The reception was empty. Tracy didn't know whether to sit and wait or seek Angel Schumer out. Desperate to question the woman and get her to open up about what she'd really meant on the phone earlier, Tracy tapped her foot, standing beside the desk, checking her watch, annoyed her appointment time would be here sooner than she'd like.

A shadow figure approached the door from the hallway, gauzy through the opaque glass. The tottering gait meant it could only be Angel, and Tracy straightened up, ready to do battle.

Angel walked in, head down, her attention on her smartphone. She smiled wide, the glow of the phone lighting up her already too-white teeth. Tracy cleared her throat. Angel snapped her head up, a squeaky "Oh!" razoring out of her, cutting the air with an irritating slice.

"You're early," Angel said, holding her phone by her side, the screen facing her body. The illumination created a rectangular patch of pink on her red pencil skirt.

"You advised me to be so," Tracy said.

"So I did. Take a seat, won't you?" Angel clip-clopped around her desk then sat, scooting her chair closer to her monitor.

"No thanks."

A flicker ticked on Angel's right eyelid.

*She's feeling under pressure.*

Tracy moved to the door, closed it, then returned to stand in front of the desk. She flattened her hands on it and leant forward. "Just what the hell did you mean earlier?"

"Be quiet. He'll hear you." Angel darted her gaze to the door.

"I don't give a shit. Tell me, or I'll speak louder." Tracy's pulse thudded at her temples. Adrenaline ran rampant, fight mode kicking in.

Angel shuddered. "He has a habit of . . . getting too comfortable with certain women. Just watch yourself. I haven't seen it for myself, but I have a sneaking suspicion he . . . *does things* when patients are under hypnosis."

"What?" That was a little loud, but it was too late now. "And you haven't done anything about it?" she whispered.

"I don't have proof."

"So install a camera!"

"I can't. It would break client confidentiality."

Tracy shoved off the desk to pace in a circle. "Oh, I'm sick of hearing that phrase. He doesn't seem too bothered about that, so why should you?"

"Because, unlike him, I actually take it seriously."

"Why are you with him? It's clear you don't like him much."

"He pays the bills. I'm staying until our children have grown."

"Good grief. I hope to God they don't know anything about your marital issues — kids deserve better than messed-up parents staying together. I understand not being able to get away from someone, I do, but get out while you can — as soon as you can." Tracy walked back to the desk, folding her arms across her middle.

"I will." Angel's expression hinted that she had something else to say but wasn't sure whether she should or not. "I . . ." She shot a glance at the door again then stood, lurching forward so her mouth was beside Tracy's ear. "I have someone. He . . . he's waiting. Only six months to go now, and our youngest will be eighteen. I'll leave then, I promise."

Tracy's previous perception of the woman vanished. "Make sure you do. Any trouble, you call me, understand?" She fished in her back pocket for one of her cards then handed it over. "I'm a police officer. I can help you."

Angel's perfect make-up was in danger of being ruined. Her eyes welled up, and she stuck the card in her bra. "Thank you."

A buzzer blared, and they both jumped.

"Fuck . . ." Tracy's heart fluttered, losing its steady beat.

Angel pressed a button below a flashing red light on a console. "Yes, Dr Schumer?"

"I'm ready for Miss Collier now."

"I'll send her right in." She jabbed the button again with a red nail tip. "Careful, all right?"

"Oh, I will be. You'd be wise to take your own advice."

Angel bobbed her head, and Tracy left her there, vulnerable and weepy behind a desk that must seem like cell bars at times. If that woman didn't get away from Dr F. soon, she'd likely end up staying for the rest of her life. It was a hard cycle to break, leaving your jailer.

At Dr F.'s door, Tracy composed herself for a few seconds, clenched her hands into fists, and took in a gulp of air. She sensed Angel's gaze on her, so turned her head and looked at her. The woman smiled — the first genuine one since they'd met — and Tracy nodded.

She faced the door and knocked, staring at the woodgrain and the gold plaque with the doctor's name on it.

"Come in," he said.

Tracy strode inside, closed the door, then walked to the green leather recliner, not the one for patients. He propped an elbow on his desk and swivelled side to side in his desk chair, a finger over his lips. He grinned, as though he'd known she would try to switch their roles. Damn it, she was a fool to think he couldn't read people from the first meeting. Of course he could — he did it for a living.

"You've made your point, Tracy — and I'll call you Tracy; much more informal in our setting. Good afternoon. Angel said you've been having . . . thoughts." He stood and moved to the coffee machine, loading the pod, placing the cup.

"Perhaps. I've always had thoughts about hurting a certain person. I suspect you know who that is. It's the delusions I'm worried about, and the hallucination. Maybe you can help me out with that. If your other patient, who we're *not* discussing, because you're not allowed to, told you all about himself, you'd know his wife — my mother — is dead. So how have I seen her through my old bedroom window? How has a member of the public identified a suspect as my mother? This is where it gets crazy and you tell me my mother *isn't* dead."

"As far as I'm aware, she is. Surely you have the means at work to check that out for yourself." He handed her a cup of coffee.

"Thank you. A death certificate means nothing. People fake their deaths." She sounded ridiculous, a drowning woman snatching at the last reed on the riverbank.

"They do. Maybe you'll never know." He set the machine to make his drink. "But it's more likely you miss her, you wished to see her, and you did. It happens. Doesn't mean you're mentally unstable. Think of all the times, for instance, when you're out and about, and you're sure you see someone, only to find it isn't them. They have the same walk, the same profile, the same hair — but they turn around and appear completely different. Yet for that split second, that one glorious moment, you saw your loved one again. I expect someone else was standing at the window." He gave her that infernal wink.

"He lives alone."

"*Does* he now . . ." He stirred sugar into his coffee then took the cup over to the patient's chair.

*What did he mean by that?* "Do you know something *I* need to know?"

"I know many things. Sadly, I can't reveal them."

She laughed. Loudly. "When it suits you, you play by the rules. I see how it is."

"Let me start by saying that I have wondered about you for many years; I've wanted to fix you for so long. The person who hurt you told me many things — things I wish he hadn't — and I want to help make them go away, to leave your head. You deserve to live a good life after . . . Well, after *that*. So, shall we start again? I'm not, and never have been, on his side. I'm merely a therapist, one who desperately wants to fix people."

"Did you fix *him*?"

"I would love to think so, but one can never be sure."

"What did you mean by saying '*Does* he now'? Has he got someone else living there? I need to know — if she's a minor, I can't allow that to continue."

"Hmm." He crossed one leg over the other. "Why hasn't that affected you until now? Because it hasn't, has it?"

*How does he know these things?*

"Because I was a selfish bitch who locked everything away and told myself I was the only one — that he only did it to me and wouldn't do it to anyone else."

"Ah, you wanted to be special." He sipped his drink, twirling his raised foot first one way, then the other.

Tracy's cheeks heated. "Doesn't everyone?" She rubbed her forehead, nudging the cup in her other hand with her elbow. Coffee sloshed and spilt on her trousers. God, that was hot. "Listen, I have so much crap in my head, you will not 'fix me'. I don't understand my reasoning — it isn't normal. I'm uncomfortable with how I've behaved since leaving that house. *Of course* he'll have moved on to someone else. *Of course* he wouldn't have stopped. He's a paedophile — he can't just switch those urges off. I've realised many things the past few days and I can't sit back in denial any longer. So, is she a minor?"

"No. Don't ask me anything else about him or her. Let's move on. Now, we've cleared up the hallucination issue. Is there anything else you'd like to discuss?"

"The delusions." She rubbed the stain on her trousers. "What are the odds that certain things in a case I'm working on match my life?"

"Expand." He frowned. Sipped. Swallowed. Sipped.

"I mean, there are specific things pertaining to the case that have happened to me or relate to me. If all four points match — that isn't normal. Two out of four, I could accept that, but not all of them. That's more than coincidence, isn't it?"

"Not necessarily. Sometimes, people pick up on things relevant to them *because* they are relevant. For example, you're online and see a pair of blue shoes. You really like them; you're considering buying them. They're in your mind, *on* your mind, and, what do you know, every time you step outside the house, you see someone wearing those shoes or similar. Those points in the case — the things they relate to are in and on your mind. Do you see? They stand out because they're a part of you, something you're not likely to forget. The fact that all four match is a long shot, but not unheard of."

He made sense, and to be honest, she was relieved to have someone tell her she'd definitely added her sums wrong.

"Right." She gulped some coffee. Scalded the roof of her mouth again. "So . . . do you think, if I'm imagining things, I should take time off work? Is that what happens when people are burnt out?"

"Some people experience strange things when tired, yes. If the case is particularly taxing, you could be overworked, not thinking straight. I would say, though, that if a fifth and sixth point turns up and relates to you . . . perhaps it needs delving into."

*Give me respite then take it away . . .*

"I want to show you something." She reached into her pocket for the folded paper then remembered she'd left it on her desk. "I would, but I haven't got it with me." *Probably for the best.* "I think the four points that relate to me are what I need to talk about. Well, three of them. I've already recalled one and thought about it, so maybe that one is dealt with."

"They're rarely dealt with just by thinking about them — unless you force yourself back there, to relive it. Have you considered hypnosis?"

*Not on your bloody life.* "No, thank you."

"That's okay. We can do this another way. You can shut your eyes, see it all in your head, and explain it to me, all the while alert and in control."

"That would suit me better."

"Finish your coffee, then we'll begin."

# CHAPTER EIGHTEEN

"Which point would you like to discuss first? I suggest you choose the one which is the most troubling to you at the moment," Dr F. said.

Tracy placed her cup on the sideboard and thought about the list. She'd dealt with the 'runaway' time by herself, and *him* talking about hanging didn't bother her at all — she'd been stronger in that episode of her life, and his words had been nothing but white noise. The fire . . . that one had upset her at Mrs Parks' flat — she'd thought she'd buried it. Clearly not. The scars from that night remained, reminding her every day what a 'worthless excuse for a human being' she was. And the rainbow scarf, the wardrobe . . .

*Oh God. They're both too much. Which one do I pick?*

"Close your eyes and allow your mind to go wherever it wants to, Tracy."

She leant her head back, placed one hand on top of the other over her crotch — she'd know if he tried anything filthy then — and did as he'd suggested, worried she'd fall asleep regardless and Dr F. would *do* things to her no matter where her hands were. Thanks to Angel's warning, she was determined to remain lucid.

No images came, her mind a blank TV screen, the episodes that made up the seasons of her life unwilling to play. Annoyed with herself for failing, she opened her eyes to find Dr F. standing in the far corner beside the door. How had he moved so silently?

Uneasy, she lifted her head. "Um, why are you over there?"

"I prefer to give a patient space. Also, some people get a little . . . angry when revisiting their past. I've been struck on several occasions." He pointed to his split lip. "Standing here, I can vacate the room faster and lock it, waiting for the patient to calm down."

His explanation was plausible.

"Okay . . ." She settled back again and closed her eyes. "It's not working."

"That's not unusual. Let me help you. Imagine a pinpoint of white light in the darkness. Focus on it and wait for it to get bigger, as though you're getting closer to it."

She did that, feeling all kinds of dickhead. It worked, though, and as the light came to within inches of her face, faint images swirled in the centre. She concentrated to make them out, but the light vanished, and she was left looking at a full scene — her old bedroom, her sight zooming to the wardrobe, and then she was inside it, back pressed into the corner, the rainbow scarf scratching her face.

"There's a man downstairs, someone I haven't met before, but *he* told me to be good and do what the new man wanted."

The creak of her bedroom door opening churned her stomach, and my God, it was like she was back there, living it all over again. She felt exactly the same — frightened, small, desperate for escape but too scared to run. He'd told her to put the scarf on — she'd never seen it before, and it smelt funny; milk vomit, musty and old. When the doorbell had rung, she'd rushed into the wardrobe to hide.

They wouldn't find her in there. They'd never guess where she was.

Someone eased open the wardrobe door. Light shone through the scarf, illuminating only the red and turquoise stripes. She peeked through the stitching, tiny gaps in the wool that afforded her a view of who stood there. Brown corduroy trousers, baggy, the knee area ballooning out where he must have been sitting at some point — maybe in the car on the way over?

She raised her gaze to his shirt — teal, flannel, grey shiny buttons, the top two undone, revealing black chest hairs. Higher still, to his neck — a thick black beard, long and scraggly beneath a loose, wet mouth she could barely make out because hairs obscured it. Thick-rimmed glasses sat on his nose, and his eyes appeared massive, but she couldn't quite see what colour they were. She shuddered, wishing she was anywhere but here. Even showing *him* love was better than this fear, this stranger, come to show her the same kind of love. How could that be? Hadn't *he* said only special fathers did this with special daughters? How come the new man was here?

"Take the scarf off," the stranger said. Was he foreign? He didn't sound right.

She didn't want to — no, she didn't want to — but did it anyway, otherwise she'd disappoint *him*.

"That's it. What a pretty girl you are."

She had no idea what this man looked like — she had her eyes shut now, tight, and she wished she could sew her eyelids together so she'd never have to see anything or anyone ever again. She'd be ugly then, and no one — not *him*, not the stranger — would want her.

"Out you come."

On hands and knees, she shuffled out of the wardrobe, the scarf whispering down her bare spine to tickle her backside. She remained on the floor, the grit on the carpet from months of it not being hoovered digging into her palms, her knees.

"Up you get. On the bed with you."

She moved on instinct, until the top of her head nudged her bed. Then she climbed up, onto the scratchy blanket, and sat, turning so she faced the door, eyes still closed.

"Look at me."

She looked — oh God, she looked — and wished she hadn't. His eyes, so brown and menacing and big, his cheeks sprouting dark hairs at random lengths — she wanted to be sick. She seemed to leave her body, floating up to the ceiling, staring down at herself and the stranger.

"Now, how about giving me that love your daddy told me you like to give."

He reached out to touch her, and she widened her eyes at a large mole the size of a penny on his inner wrist, sitting beside a scar the length of a cigarette.

Then she was in the living room, the fire inches away, the heater bars black, no heat coming from them.

"You were a naughty girl tonight," *he* said. "I told you to give the man love. You didn't give it properly. You're not supposed to cry or fight, you know that. You hurt him. He has scratches from your spiteful little nails. How is he supposed to explain them away? Do you realise his wife might suspect something? Think about that, about your actions . . . what if she leaves him? You'll have ruined her life. That poor woman will be broken, and it will be all your fault. What a worthless excuse for a human being you are, Tracy, to have done that to a happily married couple. They have children, daughters who will be destroyed by your behaviour, and all because you're a selfish cow who can't do as she's told."

Tracy shivered, still naked, her body sore — there would be bruises soon, bright purple, she reckoned, eventually fading to that murky green-yellow. Her eyes itched from welling tears.

The stranger had been mean — rough and a bully — and Mrs Wren at school said you must stand up to bullies, to people who hit you — you must try to get away if they attack you by any means necessary. She'd done that, but somehow it had been wrong. Who was right? *Him* or Mrs Wren?

"I'm going to punish you, Tracy. Stand with your back to the fire."

She did, trembling, frightened out of her mind, shaking, her bottom lip trembling. *He* came over to switch on the fire, and at first, she welcomed the heat, the way it chased away the chill in her bones, warming her, sun on her skin in the summer.

She'd had this punishment before and knew she'd have to stand there until the heat had her skin boiling, until she wanted to rip it off it hurt so much. So she stood, enduring, counting from one to whatever in her head, thinking about the last time and how she'd made it to three thousand before she'd collapsed.

Three thousand came and went. The cuckoo clock on the far wall blurted its hourly squawk. Sweat prickled on her scalp, and her cheeks seemed to want to explode, the intensity too much. She gazed through eyes swimming with tears, wanting to see *him* so she could catch his nod when he gave it — permission for her to step away, to press her back to a cool wall to soothe the pain.

He wasn't there.

She counted some more. Three thousand and fifty-two. Then, in slow motion, her knees buckled, and she went down, down, down to the floor, her mind fuzzy, registering, as she closed her eyes, that her leg pressed against the wire mesh in front of the three hot bars, the burn utterly unbearable.

Then nothing.

"When I woke up, I was in bed with a bandage on my leg." Tracy opened her eyes. "Sorry, that probably didn't make sense. I spoke at the start, then just now. You have no idea what I'm talking about."

Dr F. took three steps forward. Smiled. Clasped his hands in front of him. "But, Tracy, you told me everything. Every. Little. Thing."

What? What kind of witch-fuckery was *that*? She didn't remember telling him everything — she'd just seen it in her head, unable to form the words to match the pictures. "I . . . I don't understand."

"Amazing how it works, isn't it?" he asked, walking to the coffee machine. "I think you could do with another drink, hmm?"

She sat forward, dangling her hands between her open legs, desperate to lower her head to stop the nausea, but not wanting to once again become unaware of herself and her surroundings when in the company of Dr F.

Had he slipped something into her first coffee, was that it? Was that why she felt so sick? She was being delusional again, imagining things that hadn't happened because it suited her needs, wrapped it all up with a bright shiny bow so she could put it behind her and move on.

Worn out, she was, from remembering and from her whole life so far. How could one person carry such a burden? How could she even live with herself knowing she might have ruined the stranger's marriage?

"No. No. You didn't ruin anything. He did. The stranger did. You were a child. It wasn't your fault," Dr F. said.

She stared at him blankly, not understanding how he'd answered something she'd thought. "Did I just say that out loud?"

"Here, drink this. Take a moment to regroup. You've just been through a terrible recollection."

Even though he might not give her the answer she wanted, she asked, "Are our versions the same? Did *his* story match mine?"

Dr F. pursed his lips. He wanted to tell her — she knew it — but he didn't speak. She read his eyes — the man *did* have feelings then — and took their dampness to mean that no, the stories hadn't matched.

"I didn't think so," she said then stood.

She took two steps to the outermost point of the bay window and peered through the opaque voiles. Her car sat out there, waiting to take her back to the station, but she didn't want to go. How could she switch from this session to the case as quickly as she'd have to?

"You did very well, Tracy."

She turned.

Dr F. sat behind his desk. "I know what Angel told you. There's no need to be afraid of me. I won't hurt you, violate you, or give you any reason to be wary of me."

"Were you listening to our conversation?" Appalled, Tracy raised her eyebrows and levelled what she hoped was an expression of disgust at him.

"I'm afraid so. I have to monitor Angel closely."

"Monitor her? What kind of husband *are* you?"

He sighed, scrubbed at his face with one hand, then dropped it to his lap. "She's not very well. I wish I didn't have to say this to a patient — and sometimes I *don't* have to. Angel has specific types she latches on to, and I'm afraid you're that type."

"What are you saying? I'll tell you now, I don't like veiled comments. Just say it how it is, please."

"I'm not her husband. She's not my wife."

"So why did she tell me that then?"

"She has issues. I'm trying to aid her recovery, to ease her into normal life so she learns how to interact. Sadly, she's failing. I'm worried I can't do anything more for her. She's a former patient, Tracy — someone I want to fix."

# CHAPTER NINETEEN

Tracy left the room, heart fluttering, her get-the-eff-out-of-here response sharp and compelling, and she flew through the front door without turning to wave to Angel. She hadn't even said goodbye to Dr F., too shocked by what he'd told her. She had to put some distance between herself and him — and the frighteningly believable receptionist. Tracy prided herself on being able to read people just by being with them for a few minutes, but Angel had fooled her into thinking she was a victim, and Dr F. had at first come off as freaky and weird but had turned out to be an okay man.

Except there was still the issue of her supposedly telling him her memories with no recollection of having done so.

Was she losing her mind? Tracy was a screw-up, and since her visits to the therapist, she felt more so, not less. Would it get worse before it got better?

She sat in her car, her leg prickling, the scar burning with phantom heat like it had all those years ago. The retelling of those two incidents . . . could her body recall it, too, which was why her leg hurt now? What would it take to erase all those memories — or at least have them fade away, only surfacing if she wanted them to? She'd lived the latter for years, knowing the Past was there but not a threat anymore, then it had come knocking at her door again, begging to be let in.

Thinking back, she knew exactly when it had requested she reacquaint herself with it. The first victim being gutted had set off an alarm in her mind. That word always meant a tendril of *back then* slithered through a chink in the box she'd placed her memories in, so she shouldn't have been surprised. With Mr Quinton's account of what the woman had said to him — *Have you ever been gutted?* — she'd known, but hadn't wanted to acknowledge, that *he* hadn't let her go after all.

Sixth sense — there was something to it.

So there were five points that related to her, not four.

Gutted.

Fire.

Scarf.

Hanging.

Runaway.

She could only pray there wouldn't be any more. The issue was, she had so many 'incidents', so many things that had happened, that if he wanted to, he could go on killing for years; one murder a week for the rest of her life should cover it.

She didn't believe he was dirtying his own hands, though, so the only explanation was the woman living with him. She was the EFIT, she had to be. He was so good at controlling people, brainwashing them, that if he'd enticed the woman into his home not long after Tracy had left, he'd had plenty of time to sow the seeds and make her dependent on him. Years.

What a sick bastard.

Another thing she couldn't believe — that she'd basically solved the case already. That never happened, not so quickly. All the clues had been there from the start, and the longer time had gone on, the more information she had patched together. She had no choice but to deal with it, deal with *him* now. The Past would come to light; everything she had been through would undoubtedly spew out in court. Her team would find out. John. Kathy.

Did it matter? Really? When lives had been lost and more were at stake if she kept her mouth shut? No, it didn't matter now. And maybe that was what she needed, the whole thing blowing wide open, no more places to hide, no more secrets and lies to smother.

But not yet. She'd keep this to herself for a while longer. She'd go back to the station and talk to Damon, see what he'd done about the old lady recognising her mother. And *that* made no sense whatsoever. Had *he* chosen someone to 'love' who reminded him of his wife? She told herself she couldn't just go to his house and accuse him of murder. She had no proof, just a hunch — all based on what she wanted to believe.

She drove through the city, thinking of how she could catch him in the act without him knowing she suspected him. The only thing she came up with was to keep this part of the investigation to herself and watch him. It was dangerous and against protocol, but what else could she do? She had to stop him before someone else got killed.

* * *

"Did you follow up the EFIT information?" she asked Damon.

She sat behind her desk and smiled at him standing in front of her closed office door. He appeared tired, maybe stressed. Either way, he needed some down time, a few beers, perhaps.

"I did some digging," he said. "Your mum is definitely dead. I searched medical records, spoke to the doctor who'd attended your old home when she'd died. Definite heart attack — and your father was at his allotment when it happened. Witnesses." He shrugged. "That other woman is *not* your mother, Trace."

Relief flushed through her system, leaving her weak and with the need to go home. This day had been one of the strangest — Kathy's outburst, Angel's duplicity, Dr F. giving confusing signals so she didn't know who he was *or* his agenda. He was someone she should trust, but with his ties to *him*, she didn't think she'd ever put her full faith in the therapist. For all she knew, the pair of them could have colluded to get her to the doctor's office to screw her up even more.

*See? Is this your life now? One suspicion after another, with a gremlin at every turn that wants to see you break once and for all, your mind so frazzled you don't know who you are anymore?*

"That's something then," she managed, her voice hoarse, her throat tight from her inability to cry. If she did, Damon would know something was wrong and want to help. He'd get her thoughts out of her head in no time; she'd spill words she shouldn't spill, and he might go off in search of *him* and make a hash of things.

"Wonder who she is?" Damon pushed off the door and sat in the spare chair. "Someone has to know her."

"No idea." That much was true. Besides, she didn't want to discuss her. Damon couldn't know yet that the woman could live in the next street to where Quinton had been murdered. *Christ, so close to home.* "I need to check my emails, see if Kathy's sent anything yet. Knowing her, she'll hold on to any information for as long as possible to rub me up the wrong way."

"If she doesn't send anything by tomorrow, tell the chief?"

That was the last thing she wanted to do. She had to avoid John at the moment. She had nothing to report — nothing he'd believe anyway. "No, I'll handle it. She's just being bitchy. She's got things going on, and out of all of them, I think her dress not fitting her is top of her pissed-off pile."

"A dress? She's being a drama llama over a *dress*?" Damon frowned.

"Don't ask." She clicked her email icon. Nothing from Kathy. Nothing else she wanted to deal with either. It could all wait until tomorrow. "She hasn't sent anything. Maybe she's waiting until she's done the PM on Quinton so she can send both reports through at the same time. I suspect we'll have nothing to go on. The first two victims didn't have any prints or perpetrator DNA on them. If it's the woman doing this, she's clever." *Or she's got someone making sure she doesn't slip up.*

"Too many crime programmes on TV these days telling killers exactly what *not* to do. Honestly, they're like a how-to on murder." Damon slid his hands behind his head and curved his back in a stretch. A bone clicked. "D'you know what, I feel like we have four bodies and absolutely nothing to go on. Clean scenes, no witnesses — what the hell are we up against?" He shook his head. "By the way, I also spoke to that Martin bloke, the man Mr Parks lived with. I described the clothes Parks was wearing when we found him. Martin reckoned Parks didn't own anything like that. So whoever is doing this, they possibly dressed him in other clothes, which made him appear homeless."

Was that how *he* saw her? Homeless because she didn't live with him, because the only home he felt she should have was the one she'd grown up in? That had to be another clue. She remembered what Dr F. had said about a fifth or sixth matching point. She hoped there wouldn't be more.

"Balls. That reminds me," she said. "I need to speak to Stuart about that Lexus that was seen by the barn."

"Oh, don't bother. He found a long list. Two thousand and five of them. None of the owners have priors. Stuart went through them all, giving them a ring to ask whether they use that road or not. One does — he's a doctor, was out on call, and he was there on the morning in question. His alibi is sound — Stuart followed it up with the medical practice and the person the doctor visited."

"So we're back to square one with regards to Parks. He either walked there with the killer, or the killer drove them there. If Kathy would shift her arse, we'd have an approximate time of death and a clearer window to work with. As for the first two, we can only assume they let the killer inside their homes."

"That makes sense. Oh, and also, the prints in the houses of the first two victims — they all belong *to* the victims."

"What, *all* of them?"

"They had no family, remember, and both were loners — no friends."

Tracy gritted her teeth until they hurt. "We're up shit creek."

"For now. Something's got to give."

Tracy glanced at her watch. Four o'clock. "Sod this. Let's all go home. We're chasing our tails here. Thanks for holding the fort."

He stood. "How did it go with Dr Schumer?"

"He's good. I talked."

"That's brilliant. How do you feel?"

"Crazier than ever."

"Want to come to mine, or shall I come to yours tonight?"

"Rain check. I had a heavy session with the therapist. I need some processing time." Another lie to add to the ever-growing pile. She hated it, but she couldn't watch *his* house with Damon in tow. No, she needed to do this by herself.

Just like *he* wanted.

* * *

Tracy left her office once her team had departed. She glanced down the hallway, glad the coast was clear of John, whose office stood at the end to the right. She crept along, entering the main room with the intention of getting out without letting anything distract her. She ignored the white board, which called to her and, head down, so engrossed in her final destination, she bumped into John coming in from the other side.

*Fuck.*

"Ah, glad I caught you," he said.

John, an affable man of about sixty, who allowed Tracy to get on with things without his interference for the most part, blocked her way with his broad, stocky body. What did he bloody *want*? Surely he wasn't going to break a habit of a lifetime and start poking his nose in now.

"What do you need, sir?" she asked, forcing a smile, her nerves shimmering with irritation. She just wanted to go home, eat something, get changed, then go and sit outside *his* house.

"I wondered if you'd like to join me for a drink," he said.

She hadn't heard him right. Couldn't have. Never in the whole time they'd worked together had he wanted to socialise. Truth be told, Tracy suspected he enjoyed his status and thought it meant he should do the least amount of hard graft possible — including team-building — and wanted minimal interaction with his staff, so why the invitation?

"Can we not just discuss work here with a coffee?" Uncomfortable under his penetrating, visual examination, his eyes far too piercing for her liking, she turned her head away.

"It's not about the job, Tracy."

She whipped her attention back to him. "What *is* it about then?" She couldn't think what on earth he'd want to talk to her about.

"Can we just discuss it in the pub?" He smiled, his expression full of hope. "I'll buy you dinner, if you like."

That would work, providing he didn't keep her chatting for too long. It would save her from cobbling something together at home, most likely a Pot Noodle — food of the busy. "All right, but I've only got a couple of hours — until seven, say."

"That's plenty. Shall we?" He held out his arm.

She didn't take it. John covered his embarrassment brilliantly by scratching his elbow, as though he'd meant to do that all long.

"Which pub?" she asked, thinking it wouldn't be wise to go the Stilton Wheel — other officers might be there. She had a weird feeling about this.

"What about the Hangar? It's out of the way and quiet. Shall we go in my car?" He took his keys out of his pocket, tossed them in the air, then caught them.

"No, thank you. I'll meet you there. See you in a bit."

She strode away, needing space, the overwhelming feeling of being cornered biting at her. Leaving the building with him would be unusual and might set tongues wagging. Steeped in guilt over agreeing to meet the chief in an informal setting, she ran into the car park. She didn't have much choice in the matter, going with him, seeing as she was still technically on the clock, never mind about her overtime last night dealing with the Quinton murder.

In her vehicle, she got going straight away, heading for the Hangar on the outskirts of the city, a vast place that had once housed small, private airplanes. She didn't like it there — the food was overpriced and minimal, typical health-nut fare. She fancied steak pie and mash but doubted it would get within sniffing distance of their menu. She mourned the loss of having a Pot Noodle and told herself to be grateful she was getting to eat at all. The Past had seen many a day without food.

Sick of herself and her ungratefulness, she swerved into the car park and found a space close to the pub. Steeling herself for what was to come, she strode into the Hangar and, once at the bar, ordered a tonic water with ice.

And waited.

# CHAPTER TWENTY

John was surprisingly good company, if a little boring at times. Their conversation so far had revolved around his days as a rookie and how criminals had changed so much a copper feared for their lives most days on the street. Knife crime was a hot topic, one Tracy tried to steer him away from, seeing as her latest case involved one.

*Just a couple more days without him asking how it's going, that's all I need.*

"So, for a meal out together where you didn't want to talk about work, you've done a grand job of talking about nothing else." She laughed to take the sting from her words, ending up sounding maniacal.

"I . . . I'm nervous so babbled about what we have in common. Would you like a dessert?"

Tracy nodded. The miniscule amount of pasta she'd eaten would only have filled a child, so a good old piece of apple pie and ice cream would go down a treat. "That would be lovely, thanks." She eyed the time on a massive clock above one of several fireplaces. Six forty. He'd better get to his reason for their chat or she'd have to leave him to it.

"Got other plans tonight?" he asked.

"Yes, I'm due somewhere around seven thirty." She perused the menu, horrified to find the desserts were the type only the glamorous ate. The closest to her kind of pudding was a rhubarb something-or-other, so she opted for that, and imagined it would come out on a huge plate, the sweet the size of a golf ball, and random chocolate splashes giving the illusion she had more than she really did. She pointed to her choice. "I'll have that, thank you."

He disappeared to the bar, lost among the throng of people who had too much money to spend and nowhere better to be. Unlike her. She couldn't wait to get out of there and back to working the case.

Her phone beeped, and she took it out of her pocket.

JUST CHECKING YOU'RE OKAY, TRACE.

Damon.

She responded.

I'M FINE. DIDN'T GET TO GO HOME. JOHN WANTED TO TALK, SO WE'RE IN THE HANGAR, OF ALL PLACES. LEAVING AT SEVEN.

Damon's reply came back fast.

WTF?

I KNOW. TELL YOU ABOUT IT TOMORROW. GOT TO GO. HE'S COMING BACK FROM THE BAR.

She stuffed her phone away, for some reason blushing. John sat, placing a drink in front of her. The ice cubes clinked.

"Um, I hope that hasn't got alcohol in it," she said.

"No. Lemonade. I saw that's what you had before." He smiled.

"No, that was tonic water, but lemonade is fine. Thank you. So, can we get to the reason you wanted to speak to me, only time's running away." She took a sip, hiding a squint at the sweetness. She didn't do sugar.

"Yes, of course. Erm, I don't quite know how to start." He fidgeted, farting about with his tie, smoothing the length then rolling the end up.

It got on her nerves. "How about you just dive right in and be done with it."

She gave him a terse smile — too late to change it into a polite one; he'd caught sight of it, his eyebrows rising.

*Bugger.*

"Okay." He folded his lips over his teeth until they disappeared. "I know what happened to you, Tracy."

What. The. Hell? "Pardon?"

"Your father. He's been of interest for some time."

*Play dumb.* "What for, not trimming the grass around his allotment?"

"Tracy, Tracy, Tracy. You *know* what I'm talking about."

She shook her head. "Sorry, no. You've got me stumped."

John sighed, the exhalation hitting her face, cold and smelling of what he'd eaten for dinner with a hint of his dark beer. "It's not healthy to hide it. Your past, I mean. It isn't right to pretend, to keep it all inside."

"Keep what inside?" *Please don't bring it up. Please don't tell me you really do know what he's done. What I've done.*

"Abuse, Tracy."

Shit. So he *did* know.

"What has his actions got to do with me?" she asked, nervous and trying hard not to show it. She gulped a couple of mouthfuls of lemonade. "I left home at eighteen and never regretted it. If he's been messing around with others, that's on him. *It isn't my fault.*" Should she take some of the blame, though? After all, she'd got away, leaving him to continue his sordid behaviour on some other innocent. Or to use that woman he now lived with to act out his perverse fantasies.

"It has *everything* to do with you." John smiled tightly — a waitress had appeared, placing their desserts and spoons in front of them.

Tracy thanked her and waited until she'd walked away. "Listen to me, John. I appreciate your concern, but really, you don't need to worry on my account. If you're going after him, do so with my blessing." Were coppers already staking him out? Would that interfere with her plans to go after him herself? "There is no love—"she cringed at that word — "lost between us."

She busied herself spooning up some of her dessert then popping it into her mouth. Tasteless, it sat on her tongue — she couldn't bring herself to swallow it. John stared at her, his tiramisu untouched. Tracy couldn't handle his fixated gaze so dipped her head to focus on her plate.

There were the chocolate splashes.

She wanted to laugh.

Instead, she swallowed the lump of pudding. It stuck in her throat, and panic reared up inside her. A second later, the food went down. "I've been seeing a therapist," she said to cover her discomfort. It was something to say, and she needed to ensure he understood she was fit for duty. "It's all fine. He's getting to the crux of the problem pretty quickly, and I'm dealing with it extremely well. I've coped ever since I left home, actually, but wanted to get it off my chest once and for all anyway. You know, put it all behind me."

"You've been seeing a therapist for *yourself*?"

He appeared shocked, his mouth going slack, and Tracy swore his mind worked overtime — but why? Why would her seeing a therapist for herself matter?

"Is there a problem with that?" she asked. "Or do I need to see one of *our* therapists?"

"Oh, I was just shocked, that's all. I thought . . ." He waved his hand. "It doesn't matter what I thought. Therapists are all well and good, but seeing the same one as your father might not be a good idea."

He knew? How? "Have you had someone following me?"

"Your whereabouts have been noted at times, yes." He stopped playing with his tie and laced his fingers, elbows on the table.

*'Never put your elbows on the table, Tracy, it's bad manners. Go and stand in front of the fire.'*

She shuddered, willing the images away. To succeed at it, she forced herself to raise her head and concentrate on John — his five o'clock shadow was grey now, bordering on white. It seemed only last week it had been black sprinkled with silver.

"Right." She placed her spoon on her plate, on top of a drizzle of chocolate the shape of an exclamation mark. "I'll go and see another therapist. It's fine." She sipped her drink again, a small sliver of ice sliding down her throat. She choked for a second time, coughing and spluttering until the chip went down, cooling her windpipe along the way.

"Are you all right?" John reached over and rested a hand on hers — and stroked it.

She stood, her thighs banging into the table, their cutlery clanging, the contents of their glasses sloshing. Her mind awash with the connotations of his gesture — of unwanted touches, of improper behaviour — she blurted, "I have to go!" then hurtled towards the main doors that seemed a mile away. Her vision narrowed — the door filled the tunnel ahead of her — and she burst outside, gasping for breath and trying to battle nausea.

Shaking, she bent over, clamped her hands on her knees, and concentrated on regulating her breathing. Her attempt failed, so she straightened and peered towards where she'd left her car.

It wasn't there.

Panic fluctuated her heartbeat, and she staggered along the path outside the Hangar, checking then double-checking each vehicle. They appeared as fuzzy shapes and colours, and she cursed the way fear wreaked havoc with her mind. She'd be fine once she got home — she would — and she'd talk to Damon; he'd know what to do. She couldn't go to *his* house, not now other police officers might be there, sitting in their car a few doors away, waiting for him to do something wrong. And if she didn't find her sodding car, she wouldn't be going anywhere fast.

"Tracy? Whatever's the matter?"

She turned. John — well, the shape of him — stood in front of her. She viewed him through mist, as though tears filled her eyes, but she wasn't crying. No, she was *not* crying.

"My car . . ." She tried to lift her hand to point to where it had been, but her arm weighed too much, her fingers numb and tingling.

"Someone must have stolen it, Tracy."

Blurry John moved towards her, and instinct, some primal urge, told her not to let him near her. She stumbled to the side, unable to break her fall, and landed on the path, grit jabbing into her cheek, the same as it had on her palms and knees when she'd burnt her leg on the fire.

Lifted — she'd been lifted . . . by John? — her struggle to be free of his hold useless. Her mouth dried, her tongue seeming to expand and fill her mouth so she couldn't take in any air.

"I'll call in the theft, Tracy. You're unwell, so I'll pop you in my car, all right?"

She couldn't answer, the words unable to get out.

He carried her, calling out, "It's fine. Nothing to see here. I'm a police officer."

People must have come out to see what was happening.

Then she was lowered onto what she assumed was his back seat, and the door closed, nudging her feet. She had no energy to tuck her legs up higher and remained in an awkward position, her neck and calves cramping.

Another door shut, and she squinted through the two front seats at John, who smiled back through the gap. He had one hand on the passenger seat, his jacket and shirt sleeve showing an expanse of wrist.

A wrist with a large mole the size of a penny, sitting beside a scar the length of a cigarette.

## CHAPTER TWENTY-ONE

I'm on the hunt again, except this time I really must stick to the rules. He's created an elaborate plan — his words, not mine — and if I pull this off, I'll be set free earlier. He's decided ten is too many now, too risky, so this is my last time, my final victim.

I clutch the piece of paper. It's damp — sweat will do that — his address scribbled on it. I can't work out whether it's through fear or excitement, that damp. Both produce similar sensations, don't they, the bubbling in your tummy, the butterflies in your chest. Either way, I'm hyped up and ready to roll, my knife in the sheath, hidden from the next one's prying eyes. Until it's too late.

The house . . . I'm there now, standing outside, hidden behind the red post box perched in front of his brown, waist-height fence. I crouch a bit and peer around at the windows. No lights on upstairs, but there's a faint glow through the leaf-patterned glass in the front door, and what I'm guessing is a lamp in the front room. It's close to the cream-coloured curtains, perhaps on a small table, the nimbus of the surrounding light paler than that of the bulb, which is a bright ball.

I check the street — all clear — and stuff the paper in my back pocket. I pat my blonde wig; it's stupid, curly, and itchy.

Repositioning the clear-lens, red-framed glasses with the fake, diamond-encrusted decorations on the bridge, I'm just about ready to go. My dark lipstick will help my disguise, as will the eyeliner. *He'd* bought them all today and helped me get ready.

Heartbeat tickering faster, I pull on my gloves then step out from behind the post box and approach the front door. I knock, the sound somewhat muffled from the leather stretched over my knuckles, take a deep breath, and put on a suitably distraught expression.

The shape of a figure moves towards the door, the leaves on the glass further distorting his already ambiguous image. He swings it open, his shirt buttons undone to halfway down, chest hair on show — he has no shame, that man.

I stumble forward, connecting my hands with his chest, giving him just enough of a shove to ensure he steps backwards so I'm able to put one foot over the threshold.

"Help me! Please, help me. Some woman was chasing me." I glance over my shoulder for effect. "She . . . she had a . . . had a . . . *knife*!"

Using my weight, I push against him. He staggers farther inside, grabbing the newel post to steady himself, and I don't care because I'm completely in his house, phase one complete, just like the first two.

"Stay right there," he says, gripping my upper arms and shaking me a bit. He stares with narrowed eyes, a deep frown creasing, two ravine lines between his eyebrows. "Do *not* leave this house."

He puts the door on the latch then closes it to, and through the centimetre gap, I track what he's doing. He's down the path in no time, out onto the pavement and glancing left then right. Drawing his phone from his trouser pocket, he checks the street again. Then he's making a call, one I don't want him to make.

"Please," I whimper, opening the door wider and filling the space. "I think . . . I need your help. My heart . . ."

He turns and runs back up the path. I step back, and he dives inside, locking the door then sliding his phone away into his pocket with his back to me. I unsheathe my knife, adrenaline doing a fox trot on every nerve, pushing me on towards the promise of freedom at last.

He spins round, and I stab him in his belly, the spleen area — painful, that — and muster my strength to rip upwards, but he grips my wrist so hard it hurts. The feeling goes out of my hand fast, and I pull the knife out. It clatters to the walnut-coloured laminate flooring, skittering towards the bottom stair. A speck of blood jumps off the blade and settles on the carpet covering the step.

"What the fuck?" he says, his face paling, a nice juicy red stain spreading on his white shirt.

He twists me round, tugging my arms behind my back, and I let him think he has the upper hand. *He* warned me this man would know what he was doing, that he'd be well able to defend himself, and I have a Sharpie just for this eventuality.

"I'm sorry." I pant. "I thought . . . I thought you were the woman . . ."

His grip loosens, and I yank my hands away, spin within a millisecond, whipping the pen out of my cleavage then stabbing it into his eye. He goes down, on his knees, hands to his face, and I kick him where it hurts, my reward a guttural moan.

"Get up and get in there," I say, pointing to a door on my right, even though he probably can't even see me.

Hahaha. Hahaha.

Amazing, but he does as he's told, shuffling on his knees into a living room. Blood droplets leave a pattern behind him, random and wet, their edges jagged with where they've splashed on the hard floor. I follow that man, amused at him falling onto his side on a lovely cream rug.

"You've ruined that," I say. "Nice bit of home furnishing, that. Or it was."

He grunts.

"What was that?" I step closer, standing in front of him. "Couldn't quite hear you. Anyone would think you'd been stabbed in the stomach and eye."

Laughter isn't far away. I hold it back — time for cracking up later — and kick his shin with my hard, brown boot. The laces have come undone, one of them resting over his bare foot.

He moves his head, looks at me with his good eye. The other is closed, bulbous, the bruise coming along nicely. I'm proud of my damn self.

"Now, you're going to do as you're told, okay?" I wait for his nod. "You're losing quite a bit of blood from your belly, so if I were you, once you've done what I ask, you should keep as still as possible. Now, roll onto your back."

He does.

Then I stomp on his face repeatedly until he blacks out.

# CHAPTER TWENTY-TWO

Tracy drifted off on the journey, barely aware of anything but her inner self. She'd swear she was only her soul — the thinking, feeling part of her — her body useless and unresponsive.

The image of that mole and scar floated in her mind, taking her back in time, to when she'd focussed on those two things instead of what he'd been doing. A thick, black, wiry hair had protruded from the mole, curling at the end, and it had reminded her of a pig's tail. The scar resembled a ragged cut, a serrated knife perhaps used to slice his skin — by his hand or another's?

Their conversation at the Hanger repeated itself then, where he'd boasted of apprehending a suspect despite being stabbed. In the arm, he'd said; hadn't been specific as to where. He'd bragged that not many officers would be able to cuff a suspect while blood spurted out, but he had. Now, she wondered if he'd been trying to tell her something or make her think he was someone amazing. Ego issues?

Too tired to work it all out, she dozed again, then woke, still groggy but not as much as before. Streetlights passed every so often — a residential area, then, further proved by the sound of a street crossing bleeping, and she imagined the green man flashing. The car slowed, and she struggled to raise herself so she could alert someone outside that she needed help.

She may as well have been packed full of lead.

Tears burnt, and she was glad, thankful her body still worked to some degree. She closed her eyes, shutting out the signs of the world beyond the vehicle, frustrated at being incapacitated, vulnerable — and out of control. That was the worst part.

The car moved off again, and instead of thinking about where the hell he was taking her — surely they'd travelled miles — she picked at her memories since working with John, trying to figure out why she hadn't recognised him. It must have been the long black beard and glasses back then throwing her off — she'd kept his image in her head from childhood, and as she'd grown, she'd vowed she'd never forget what he looked like, so one day, she'd get even with him. But it hadn't worked out that way. His accent all those years ago, she now knew to be French. He'd faked it all so he wouldn't give himself away, and then, when he'd met her later in life, he'd pretended he was someone completely different.

What *he* had said, about the stranger's wife finding out . . . she couldn't have. John had been married to Brenda for forty years — that's what John had told her, and she'd had no reason not to believe him. *He* had lied to her, and all this time she'd blamed herself for wrecking a marriage that had lasted until this day.

How did *he* live with himself? How did John? Didn't they care? And how the hell had they met each other? A paedophile club? Without the internet at that point, how had they arranged meetings?

Had John remembered their encounter when he'd found out her name after she'd joined his division? Or hadn't he known who she was? Better for it to be an anonymous child he'd—

She wanted to see Damon, for a hug that would take every bad thing away. And, bizarrely, she wanted to see Dr

F. Was he in on this, too? Had everything been planned to lead up to this moment? *He* had arranged the recent murders, she had no doubt of that now. He'd been warning her he was coming for her, and she hadn't believed the signs until it was too late.

Had John known somehow that she was closing in on *him*?

Then it struck her: Dr F. It was clear John had thought she was seeing him *because* of her father. Questioning him. She'd been innocent, dragged into this shitstorm through no fault of her own. So again, thoughts of whether Dr F. was involved, whether he'd been sent to the coffee shop on purpose, ricocheted through her mind. Was that why he'd deliberately swiped his business cards off the table? To force a connection — and all three of them — Dr F., *him*, and John, had to just hope she or Damon took the bait?

No, too far-fetched.

Wasn't it?

She didn't know anymore. People were capable of anything if they set their mind to it. Everything was possible.

The car stopped, yanking her out of her mind and into the present. John opened his door and got out. She held her breath, straining to hear something that might give her a clue as to where he'd taken her. Nothing but the scuffle of John's feet on a path, maybe, a few skittering meteors of grit bouncing.

He flung open the door at her feet, climbing in, looming over her. Oh God, was he going to repeat his actions from when she'd been a child?

*No, please no. No that . . .*

She glared at him, eyes wide, and moved — actually moved — but only a little, enough to draw her knees closer to her belly. Then she shifted her arms, covering her chest, elated by such a simple thing she'd taken for granted since she'd left *him* — protecting herself from men who wanted to take what wasn't theirs. This couldn't be happening, not again. Not after all the years she'd managed to stay safe.

"Remember this, Tracy?"

He brought something out from behind him. An illusion, it had to be. The interior light splashed onto what he held up, and she zeroed her attention onto two colours — red and turquoise.

*The scarf. He has the damn scarf.*

She whimpered, angry at herself for showing weakness, but this was too much. She'd carved a safe life out for herself, only to come full circle.

"Put it on," he said. "Like before."

"I can't." Her words, thick and gloopy, sounded alien — not her voice. "I can't . . . move."

"But you just did. I saw you."

"Too tired now."

He sighed — again with the food and beer breath — and her stomach churned. Sliding the scarf beneath her head, he then placed it over her eyes and tied it above her temple. Hot air fanned her mouth, and she knew from so much experience, his mouth hovered above hers.

*Don't you dare . . .*

She wanted to be sick and managed to turn her head so his heated breath seared a patch of her jaw. Bile burnt her throat, and she swallowed it back down, refusing to give him any other indication that he revolted her — and that she was scared. So, so scared.

She sensed him leave her, his oppressive, suffocating presence gone. The car rocked, then his disgusting sausage-fingered hands grasped her ankles, and he pulled.

She fell out onto a hard surface, pain smarting her hip, and closed her eyes, scrabbling to sit upright, making a piss-poor job of it. She allowed herself to settle on the ground and swept her fingers over it — either a path or a driveway — yet something wasn't right. She opened her eyes, squinting through the tiny holes in the wool, the light from the car not enough to illuminate anything beyond the vehicle.

Was that a grey breeze-block wall. Were they inside a garage?

"Get up," John said.

He lifted her to her feet and, hating herself for having to, she leant into him while he dragged her along. Up two steps, then through a doorway — she made out the jamb, over-painted in white gone cream-coloured with time, the light from the room they entered stark and piercing.

*Where the hell am I?*

Her eyes glazed over.

"Over here," he said, tugging her across what felt like carpet.

He let her go, and she fell backwards, landing on something soft yet with a hardness on it, reminding her of Mrs Parks' home, the magazine crackling as she'd sat.

"Now then, it's time to wait," he said. "I'm going to make a cup of tea. Don't you be going anywhere." He roared with laughter, then his footsteps indicated he'd left her.

*Thank God.*

Time passed slowly. At one point, she must have fallen asleep, as she jolted awake at a noise, a ticking, one she recognised. Fear and panic collided inside her, creating a maelstrom of emotions that turned her inside out and wrung her dry.

What she'd heard couldn't be possible.

It sent her right back to the Past.

Heat, heat on the back of her naked body.

Counting into the thousands then . . .

*Cuckoo . . . cuckoo.*

# CHAPTER TWENTY-THREE

Dr George Schumer sat at his desk, staring at the closed blinds to the far left over the bay window, his desk light flashing every so often — the bulb was on its way out; it buzzed with the last flickers of life, an angry wasp. He'd been in the same position for a long time, wishing he could get up. Wishing he'd stood beside the door in the corner so he could have vacated the moment his patient had gone off on one.

Angel, sprawled in the centre of the floor, half on and half off his Oriental rug, had stopped breathing just after eight o'clock. Her pink blouse had been torn open, one pearlescent domed button hanging by a wiggly thread. Blood stained the blouse — a large patch and several splotches — and it also marred her stomach skin — the skin that had once held it all together, skin that now gaped. A pool of red had soaked into his rug, creating the shape of a cumulus cloud. At one time he would have lamented the mess, the price he'd paid for the carpet, now ruined. But not tonight. Tonight it didn't matter. All that mattered was him getting out of this alive, using every one of his skills to calm his patient and convince him this wasn't one of his better choices in life — not that he'd made many good ones.

With Angel's mouth and eyes wide open, from this angle, him studying her from the head down, she appeared as a human-sized doll, placed there by a deranged man who not only liked little girls but also getting his own way.

George conceded defeat. He hadn't fixed him. He'd failed. And what of Angel? He'd almost pieced her broken mind back together. She'd only had the lying left to combat, and then she'd have been set to live a good life, an easier life than the one she'd endured since a terrible incident in her twenties. All those lies of hers would have been gone, given another year. And now she'd never utter another.

His patient sat in the green leather chair, just like his daughter had, wanting to be the one to control the session. George could only hope this meeting went the same way as Tracy Collier's had, the tables being turned, and him in the driving seat.

Somehow, though, he doubted it would work this time. David Collier was in another dimension, focussed on only one thing — teaching his child a lesson.

Wrists chafing on the rope that bound them behind his back, George longed for the next step — even though he feared it. He knew, when dealing with David, to take it slow, to let him direct the way things would go. Time was running out, though. He had no doubt whatsoever that Tracy was where David had said she was, and her boyfriend was in the hands of the woman David lived with.

A shiver ran up and down George's spine, and he resisted giving a visible reaction to it. Wouldn't bode well for him to show his fear. David thrived on seeing it in any form; he'd said so many years ago during their appointments.

"Where *is* she?" David muttered.

"Who, David?" The therapist method would be best — it was what David really needed, after all. That steadying influence, someone to steer him right. George had believed for all these years he *had* steered him right. How wrong he'd been.

"Her. She should be here by now."

*Someone else is coming here?*

Acting a sandwich short of a picnic, George said, "Now you *know* where Tracy is, David. She's at home, where she belongs." *God help me for lying.*

"Not *that* one," David snapped.

"Oh, I see. Do you feel happier, more settled now you know Tracy is back at home?" He'd keep him talking about the daughter who had filled his mind for fourteen years of separation — and the eighteen before that.

"Yes, of course I bloody do. I've missed her. Missed her love."

George's stomach twisted, and he wondered, for perhaps the millionth time, why he'd chosen this profession, where people came to him to spill their sordid, disgusting secrets, and he was supposed to fix them. You couldn't fix a paedophile. He'd been a naive fool to think he could. "I'm sure you have. As you stopped coming to see me a short while after she left, tell me, how have *you* been? It's important to me that I know you're all right." *It's important to me to know your state of mind.*

"Been figuring out ways to get her back. To bring her home." David shrugged, a surly child in an old man's body.

"And this plan, the one you told me about when you first came here tonight, that's the only way, do you think?"

"Nothing else worked. I sent her letters, loads of them, and John swears he gave them to her — I sent them to the station, see — but she ignored them all. She's too much like her mother — not good with taking orders or doing what I want. That's why her mother had a heart attack, you know."

"She had a heart attack from not following rules?"

"Yes. She disobeyed me one too many times. Had the cheek to tell me my love for Tracy was wrong, didn't she, so I showed her. I made sure she had that heart attack."

Client confidentiality was a bastard.

Getting the gist of what David had said, George couldn't bear talking along those lines anymore. "Do you think perhaps John *didn't* give the letters to Tracy? Maybe he worried about the contents and how it would affect him. What was in the letters? Would you like to unburden yourself, let all the tension bleed away?" He cringed at his word usage and glanced at a crimson-coated Angel.

Her guts, piled on the rug beside her, had him retching.

"I wrote and told her who John was," David said. "That he'd loved her before and would love her, in my place, until we could be together again."

George swallowed and composed himself. Shifted his gaze from Angel to David. "I see. So it would make sense for her *not* to get the letters." He was playing a dangerous game, goading David, but if he could get the man's attention and rage on someone else, the odds might go in the George's favour.

David narrowed his eyes. "That bastard . . ."

"Hmm. It seems he's been less than truthful with you. More lies, David. More people lying to you." *Please, God, let this work.* "Would you mind untying me? My wrists are sore, and I'm sure you'd like me to make you a coffee. Like the old days, eh?"

"*You've* never lied to me," David said. He stuck out his bottom lip.

"No. No, I haven't." *Until tonight.*

David rose then shuffled over, his gait belying his strength — strength he'd used to overpower George and tie him up, and to kill Angel, a slice to her stomach, then the wrenching of the knife, up and down, up and down, until everything had come tumbling out of her.

George held his breath while David stood to the side of him and untied the rope. Immediate relief came, and George slowly inched his hands in front of him to rub at the red skin. Then, while David walked away, he slid one hand behind him to feed the rope inside his waistband.

"Thank you," George said. "Now, sit yourself down, and I'll make a coffee, then we can talk properly, all right?"

David nodded, appearing a little bewildered for a second, only for the mask to come back over his face — a scowl, slitted eyes, his mouth a grimace. "I'm sick of everyone playing me for a fool." He slumped into the green chair.

George stood and carefully picked his way across to the coffeemaker, ill at ease with David sitting so close and a dead Angel behind him. The door was locked — no sense in making a run for it. For an old man, David was extremely spry when he had a mind.

"You like plenty of brown sugar, don't you, David?"

"Yes. And strong. So the spoon could stand up in it."

Dr Schumer fitted the pod and set the machine to work. He shuddered at the familiar answer and wondered whether Tracy had heard the same thing over and over during those terrible years she'd lived with her father. His wife had heard it, Dr Schumer would bet — had probably wanted to throw the damn coffee over his pasty, sallow skin a time or two. "Here you are." He held the cup aloft.

David turned to take it, and Dr Schumer launched the contents at him, the scalding liquid pouring over David's face. David let out a roar of anger and pain, and Dr Schumer dropped the cup and reached behind to take out the rope. He secured it around his patient's neck, pulling tight so David tipped forward onto the floor, inches from Angel's outstretched arm, her polished fingernails pointing at her killer.

Clutching at the rope, scrabbling ineffectually to loosen the constricting hold, David writhed. George dragged David towards him, the man's back to his shins, his head resting on his thighs, and tugged harder. He glared down at the man he'd despised from day one, at the face no longer sallow but bright red, and told himself he was doing this for all victims — not just Tracy. George's arms ached — he wasn't sure he could hold on for much longer.

David went slack. His eyes closed, but his chest still rose and fell. The idea of actually taking a life flew through George with harsh wings, and he relaxed his grip, thinking to tie David up then press the panic button under his desk, which would alert the police.

*Why didn't I do that after he'd untied me?*

He could have slapped his forehead, but now wasn't the time.

He dropped to his knees, David's upper body and head lolling on George's thighs, and shoved him off, over onto his side, his arms conveniently behind him. He snaked the rope under one of David's wrists, holding his breath and willing himself to get a move on before the man regained consciousness.

Too late, David rolled super-fast and was up on his feet inside a blink, a new mask in place now, one George had never seen before. It was of a man possessed, all gleaming eyes and spittle-flecked lips, the muscles in his jaw flexing, dentures clenched.

George backed away, feeling blindly for his desk, then scooting behind it to reach beneath and press the button. David advanced and, with incredible speed, whipped out the knife he'd used to kill Angel and held it out in front of him.

George thought about the times he'd messed with people's minds, all because he'd enjoyed watching their reaction. He'd done it to Tracy in the coffee shop, and to David, too, just a few minutes ago when riling him about John and the letters.

He didn't feel so smug now. Not when the knife painlessly entered his stomach, then a tearing agony coming soon after with the knife's upward progression.

"Have you ever been gutted?" David whispered.

George went down. He hit the floor, the breath knocked out of him, and rolled to his side, clutching his belly. His thoughts made an unholy mess in his mind, an angry scribble, each one overlapping the other, a host of memories resembling a nest of snakes.

He had tried to fix snakes, had been a snake himself at times, and never in all his years had he thought his last image would be of a woman he'd wanted to mend but couldn't. As he closed his eyes, he prayed Tracy would find someone else to patch her up.

Providing she got out of this alive.

# CHAPTER TWENTY-FOUR

I tied him up and left him on the rug. He's not dead — the intention never was to kill this one. No, he has to live so he has a constant reminder when he gawps in the mirror at his pulpy face or down at his ripped belly, that he loved someone he shouldn't have. Someone who has always belonged to someone else. That's his punishment for being with *her*, the one who upset *him* so much. Me, too.

I can't bring myself to feel even an ounce of affection for her.

Silly little bitch — she ruined everything from the moment she was born.

I hate her and I love her.

I'm nearly at Dr Schumer's now — my, it's a long walk. *He* never told me that. Said I'd arrive there 'in no time'. If no time is over an hour, then he needs to rethink his idea of how long journeys take on foot. He's used to driving the Lexus, the one he stores in the garage. He'd bought it from a scrap dealer, who'd promised to send in the paperwork to say it had been crushed if *he* promised to use a different number plate.

The last time I was in it was when he'd picked me and Number Three up. He'd taken us to the barn, had left me while I'd done my thing, then helped me hoist the silly dead bastard up, into one of the positions he's most insistent on. We'd left the area around two in the morning — God, I'd been exhausted.

The last position, of *her* boyfriend, will really put the shits up her and make her understand who she's dealing with. That no amount of running will erase the past — memories go with you, constantly there, under your skin, in your head, and buried deep in your marrow. They're like your DNA, making you who you are — the traits, the characteristics, governing how you behave for the rest of your life, each spiral in the link defining you, forcing you to live by its rules.

There's no running.

That stops me walking. I stand beside Know Your Plaice — *'Get down in that basement, you little cow; know your place'* — a chip shop, to think about it, the smell of vinegar heavy on the air, taking me back to the one and only time we had a holiday. Morecambe, it was. We'd eaten sausage and chips straight out of the paper, sitting on the sea wall, the white gulls with grey wingtips swooping down, their cries from lurid yellow beaks ear-splitting. *He'd* had a pot belly by then, and Mum's had been just the same, except hers wasn't from food and beer.

No, there's no running. I've just proved it by thinking of *back then*. Wherever I end up going, whoever I'm with, I'll forever be connected to the past, which will infect my future, an abscess I can't pop.

I continue on, telling myself if I see Dr Schumer in a therapist-patient setting, like *he* promised, if I can talk to him, he'll make everything all right again.

There's a spring in my step now, and I stride faster — can't wait to get to the end of this road and step onto a new path, metaphorically, not literally. It might take me left, right, or straight ahead, but I'm never going to let it take me backwards.

Here we are; here's the good doctor's office.

The Lexus is parked out front at a slant. There are blinds drawn at the windows, and a tree stands to the right, probably protected by a conservation order, going by the size of it. It's silent here apart from the shuffling of leaves as the wind tickles them.

I reach the front door and, gloves snug over my hands, I knock.

*He* opens the door, blood splatters all over him, even on his face, a large one on his earlobe. He'd said he wasn't going to hurt anyone, that there wasn't a need for it during this phase, but it seems he's lied again. How come it's okay for him to kill now? Why did he use me for all the others?

"Get in," he says. "We need to talk."

*D'you think?*

I step inside, and he locks the door behind me. I follow him into a room with two dead people on the floor. A woman — *who the fuck is she?* — and the good Dr Schumer. Both have been gutted.

I walk over to a green leather chair and sit. "What have you done?"

"I'd have thought that was obvious, you stupid cow."

"But why? You said—"

"I know what I said, but things took a dark turn, didn't they."

It's dark all right — the blood is drying black-brown on the woman already.

"What should we do?" I ask, as always, waiting for his direction. How am I supposed to survive by myself if I can't make the simplest of choices? He's an enabler — he's allowed me to be dependent on him, doing everything for me, making life choices for me, even directing the killings.

"I need to get back home," he says. "*She's* there with John."

He's talked about John before. They're best friends, have known each other since they were kids, so *he* told me.

*So why have I never met him?*

"Will I have to see her?" I don't want to. I thought I'd be all right with it before, but now it's happening . . . Can I face his little girl, the one he favours, the one who got away? Can I stand to see him fawning over her, casting me aside?

"I think it's best you don't, now I come to think of it. You should collect your bags and leave, like we planned. I bought you a train ticket, though; it's in the outside pocket of your suitcase. You're free."

"But yesterday you said I could take the car, said those driving lessons you gave me could be put to good use. You laughed about it." I'm a small child, whining to get my own way, but when you're promised something after the upbringing I've had, you hold on to it with such hope, it's as if your whole life depends on it. He's broken another promise — me getting help from Dr Schumer — and rage builds, surging up my windpipe ready to spew out as nasty words if I don't get a hold of myself in time.

"No, *I* need the car," he says. "Plans have changed. I have to leave with *her* — I can't stay around here anymore. Not now John—"

My stomach plummets. My whole body goes cold, and my skin is clammy. "Not now John what?"

"John has been lying to me — Dr Schumer told me."

I laugh. I'm starting to see clearly. See things I knew were always there but have been taught not to acknowledge. All those times watching TV, I've learnt that what he's been doing is wrong, and the conditioning he's put me through isn't normal. Doesn't he see that *everything* has been a lie? That all of us stuck in this mad story are liars? We've had to be, to cover up for him, so he can live the life he wants.

Pawns, that's what we've been, and that knowledge smacks into me so hard it's like I've been punched. I flop back from the impact, everything I've ever known and believed smashed to pieces — although I can't claim total innocence; I knew, deep down, that all this was hideous. Especially from when I had to live in the basement.

I've been controlled, brainwashed, taught to think on his terms and obey whatever he says. If I didn't, I got hurt, but after the hurt came the love and the 'I'm sorry'. The 'I'll never do it again'.

I'm his wife, albeit one kept in the shadows, a woman who doesn't exist anymore because he made it so. Hid me for the most part, only letting me out when it suited him.

I should have run when I had the urge that time. Should have told the shop keeper what's been going on and allowed her to telephone the police.

Don't I deserve better than this? As his second spouse, don't I deserve something from this terrible mess?

*You're not married. Stop pretending you are.*

*But he said we were. That man performed a ceremony.*

*You can't be his wife, you just can't.*

*Go. Away.*

*And if you're his wife, why do you want to be free? Aren't you more like* her *than you think? Aren't you a broken bird who needs to fly? If you weren't, you'd want to stay with your 'husband'.*

"Do you love me?" I ask.

He sighs. Jams his hands on his hips while looking from Dr Schumer to the woman. Admiring his handiwork, probably wishing he'd killed all the others himself, too. "No. I never did. Now piss off. Go on! You can hang for all I care, just get out!"

I've heard similar words before, shouted by him when *she* left.

Rage, unlike anything I've experienced before, boils up and spills over, and the words I want to say twist into a braid-like strand, rising from my belly and onto my tongue, where they settle, unspoken. I remember what he said to me all those years ago after *she'd* gone, after I'd asked him why he'd been so upset: *Have you ever been gutted?* And now I understand what he'd meant. He'd been telling me *he* was gutted — gutted at her walking out on him, gutted that the 'love of his life' had chosen to spend hers without him in it. And now I feel the same way as her.

I don't want him in my life either.

*That's* why I have no problem being set free.

I stand then sidle close to a sideboard with a coffeemaker on top, covering the bloodied knife there with my gloved hand, and wait for him to finish inspecting the bodies of the people he's killed — innocent people, just like the poor souls I've snuffed out. I'd done it for him, to make him love me more than her, and it had been pointless — he'd used me to bring her back, and in the process, is letting me go. I'm not needed anymore — he'd only wanted to love me again when she'd gone for good anyway. I'm surplus to his requirements.

"I don't love you either," I say.

He stares at me, clearly unable to believe I had the balls to say such a thing. That it's impossible not to love him, considering the 'love' he's showered on me. But that kind of love was never mine, wasn't something I should ever have had, yet he'd given it to me time and again until I'd believed it was legal, that he was my one and only. My husband.

The knife slices into him, his belly against my hand, the hilt submerged halfway. His eyes widen — he can't comprehend what I've done, and a part of me can't comprehend it either. This man has been my life, my reason for living, the person I wanted to please for so many years, and for what? To be cast aside once *she* came back?

Earlier, I had no affection for her. Now, there's an inkling of compassion. We are the same, she and I, and I'll at least say sorry to her before I go.

I finish the job on him — up down, up down — and he collapses on top of Dr Schumer, one hand falling on the woman's breast. I shudder and move it away so even in death he can't touch someone when he shouldn't. Knife tossed down on the floor, I wipe my glove off on his shirt then root around in his pockets for the car keys.

I take them and leave the room, the building, my face awash with tears for the lies I believed and the lies I've told — to others, but most of all, to myself.

In the Lexus, I start the engine then pull out onto the road, turning left and heading for home. In my rearview, flashes of red and blue fill the mirror, and I hope they're not coming after me. Not now, not when I'm almost free.

The police vehicle turns into the doctor's car park, and I know I've been blessed by someone 'up there' watching over me.

Maybe, just maybe, it's my mother.

# CHAPTER TWENTY-FIVE

"Fuck. *Fuck*!"

John's voice floated towards Tracy from far away. She shook her head to clear it of sleep then opened her eyes, yanked the scarf off her face, her arm working almost as it usually would, and threw the woollen thing away from her.

The living room was exactly as she remembered it, the fire wearing a coat of dust, the fake coals above the three heater bars grey with it. She didn't shiver, didn't entertain any fear upon seeing it. What had happened had been *his* fault, and she was buggered if she'd take any blame. She'd been a child and he an adult. And those scars — she wouldn't view them as him forever imprinted on her body now but marks to show she'd survived, a badge she'd wear proudly instead of hiding them from judging eyes. Damon didn't mind them, so why should she?

Damon. Her phone.

She tapped her back pocket — it wasn't there. She shouldn't be surprised. John would have taken it away from her at some point while she'd slept. Oddly, given the circumstances, she chuckled at the thought of him seeing her latest messages about him. Then again, what if he'd gone to find Damon while she'd been dozing?

"Not her. Please, not her . . ."

What was John ranting on about now?

He flew into the room, grabbed her arm, and tugged her to her feet. She wavered, letting him think she was still groggy from whatever the hell he'd put in her lemonade.

"Come with me," he said, leading her from the room and out into the hallway to the door that led to the basement.

She'd never been allowed in there as a child. *He'd* said his 'private thing' was down there, one of his possessions, and she should never, ever ask to see the room.

She hadn't.

John swung the door open, the other side of it some kind of metal, and Tracy frowned. He pushed her in the back, and she stumbled forward, stopping herself in time — she could have hurtled down the steps.

He flipped a light on, and down the wooden stairs she went, surprised to find a furnished room, complete with a bed area to the right, a living space in the middle, a wall dedicated to a kitchen on the left, and a door beside that she assumed led to a bathroom. Curtains at the narrow window near the ceiling hadn't been drawn, the glass painted with hasty, patchy strokes. She recognised the armoire as her mother's, a great hulking brown thing with carved diamonds climbing up the centre of each door. Her mother's patchwork quilt covered the single bed, the squares of material faded since she'd last seen it, bright purples now lilac, reds turned into rose pink. Nostalgia built up as a lump in her throat, and she swallowed, the action painful.

John stood at the top of the stairs, the door almost closed, and he stared through the gap into the hallway. Wanting to speak but daring not to, she waited to see what would happen next.

"Where are you?" a woman sing-songed.

The EFIT woman? The one who lived with *him*?

John didn't answer.

"I know you're here. You'd better not be in my room, otherwise I'm going to be pissed off. That's *mine* and always has been."

Footsteps sounded overhead — the woman had gone into the living room. Then more, where she'd come out and took the steps to the second level. Tracy bit her lip, keeping her breathing shallow so she picked up as much sound as possible. John glanced down at her and raised his finger to his lips.

*Why?* she wanted to shout. *So that nutter up there doesn't find you and kill you?*

"Shit!" He scrabbled down the stairs, tripping on the last one and shooting forward to land on his hands and knees.

The basement door opened, and the same woman she'd seen at her old bedroom window peered down at her, the EFIT such a good likeness Tracy shuddered. She was young, this woman, too young for her father, but that was none of Tracy's business if the lady liked older men.

The woman switched her attention to John. "Who the hell are *you*?"

John got to his feet, his portly body swaying. "I'm a friend of your dad's. John."

She cocked her head, eyeing him intently, and descended the stairs, her thick-soled shoes clonking. At the bottom, she stood directly in front of him and sniffed. Her eyes widened, and her cheeks paled.

"You!" she said. "It's you."

"Lisa, it's okay," John said, holding out his hand. "I won't hurt you. I'd never hurt you."

"I'm too old for you now, aren't I, so of course you won't *hurt* me," Lisa said, a sneer curling her upper lip.

*He'd 'loved' her, too?*

"Lisa, please. Don't torment yourself." John took a step forward then stopped, lowering his hand.

"You had a black beard before. Glasses." Lisa shuddered. "But I'd remember the smell of you anywhere. And that scarf."

*Oh God . . .*

"I saw it in the living room," she went on. "Do you carry it around with you everywhere, you sick bastard?"

John scrubbed at his hair. "It isn't what you think. That scarf belonged to my daughter, but I couldn't . . . I never—"

"No," Lisa said, "you just fucked someone else's daughter instead."

Tracy longed to sit on the bed, but her legs, too stiff to move, meant she had to remain in place. This woman who resembled her mother had been abused, too, by the same man. *He* had provided the children, and John had taken the love without a care in the world.

Lisa slapped him, good and hard, so hard he staggered backwards. Tracy couldn't believe this woman's strength — she seemed too small to smack someone that forcefully. John held his cheek, his eyes darting left and right, and Tracy sensed his police training had kicked in. He'd been behind a desk for so long, she wasn't sure he'd remember anything worth shit, though — and she wasn't about to help him if things went tits up.

"You shouldn't have done what you did to me," Lisa said. "*He* shouldn't have done it. I was a kid, just a kid! What makes you think you have the right to do that?"

*What?*

Confused, Tracy looked from John to Lisa, dying to speak but playing the drugged-up captive for now. The time would come for her to strike — and she'd do it without question.

"He loved you and Tracy, don't you understand?" John's tone was that of a pleading child. "You're his girls, his babies. He wanted me to share that love."

*Babies?*

"A man shouldn't *love* his children any more than he should farm them out for others to love." Lisa's bottom lip wobbled.

Her terminology was the same as Tracy's — had Lisa been brought into the home and kept down here? Was that what had happened? Did she have a family out there somewhere, thinking she was a missing person, possibly dead in a ditch in the middle of nowhere, when in reality she'd been here all along?

"David Collier is a bastard — *was* a bastard," Lisa said.

*He's dead?*

"And he deserves death. Actually, no. Death was too quick, too much of an instant release. He should have been made to suffer. To be locked up, same as me."

Despite Lisa's upset, happiness soared inside Tracy, filling her up until she thought she'd burst from it. She'd long ago realised she'd never be free of that man until he was dead, and now, the heavenly sensation of every bad thing she'd ever carried floated away — all he'd done to her, all he'd said, rising, rising, leaving her clean and pure, ready to start again with no more fear he'd turn up unexpectedly and do her harm.

"What have you *done*?" John said then groaned, covering his face with his hands.

"He killed Dr Schumer and a woman. He lied to me. He said Dr Schumer would fix me. *Now* where am I supposed to get help?" Lisa raised her eyebrows. "Where is *she* meant to get help?" She poked a finger in Tracy's direction. "We're his *daughters* — we deserve more than he ever gave."

The room spun. Tracy flashed her hands out to balance herself, her equilibrium shot, her head fuzzy and her body floppy. She stepped backwards, her calf hitting the bed, and she dropped onto the quilt.

"I . . . I didn't know," Tracy managed.

"Of course you didn't. I was kept down here." Lisa waved as though her bombshell was of no consequence. "You came along, and he had a younger girl to groom."

"Mum never said . . . never told me I had a sister." Tracy's mouth went dry, and swallowing hurt.

"*He* told her I ran away, and as for this piece of shit" — she jerked her head at John — "he covered it up at the police station, just like you covered up at my killing scenes, right, John?"

"*Oh* no . . . No!" Tracy stood, the shock noodling her legs exchanged for pure anger — ripe, rancid, the type that made someone kill another. "You *knew*?" She glared at John, who removed his hands from his face and puffed his chest out. "You cleaned the damn scenes, didn't you? You assigned all these killings to me — *not* the other team. You *wanted* me on them. Why?"

"He wanted you to see the clues, to make you come back home." John clenched his hands into fists. "And I thought you knew it was him, thought you'd gone to Doctor Schumer because of it, so we had to do something to shut you up — you wouldn't have come home by yourself; we had to persuade you."

"*Persuade* me? You drugged and *abducted* me. You're out of your goddamn mind." Tracy rushed at him, shoving his chest, her anger spilling over, boiling her bones, her muscles, her skin.

He careened backwards, ending up on his arse, an *oof* coming out of him, spittle following to splat on his hand. Tracy landed on top of him, pushing him down to the floor and sitting astride him.

"Hold down his hands," Tracy said.

Lisa dropped to her knees beside them and leant over, dragging his flailing arms up and pinning his wrists down above his head with one hand. John bucked and writhed, but Tracy remained in place, rage giving her strength and determination. He kneed her in the back, sending her forward, close to his face. Revolted, she slid down to sit on his thighs.

"Have you ever been gutted, John?" Lisa asked.

Tracy's stomach muscles contracted. John's eyes bulged, the whites covered in sprawling red veins, and his lashes fluttered. He knew what she meant — he had to if he'd been in on this from the start. Tracy glanced at Lisa, who held a blood-stained knife aloft in her free hand, the red on the blade smeared and dry, the crimson matter on the hilt congealing.

"Put it down," Tracy said. "You don't want to do this."

"Oh, but I do." Lisa smiled.

"No more," Tracy said. "You've endured enough. Don't put yourself through this again."

Lisa placed the knife on the floor then took off her right-hand glove, using her teeth to pull at the fingers. She handed it to Tracy.

What her sister was asking was wrong but so significant Tracy accepted the glove and put it on. "You need to leave," she said. "Take your bags over there and go."

"What?" Lisa whispered.

"Please. Go. Just . . . go. Don't contact me once you get to where you're going. If I don't know where you are, I won't have to come and find you, will I?"

Lisa frowned. "What about his arms? He'll hurt you if I let go."

"Tuck them under my knees. Let me move up just a bit."

Lisa obeyed, and Tracy wondered if the woman was better at taking orders than making her own decisions. She identified with that — it had taken years to shake *him* off, to understand she could choose her paths in life without *his* permission. Lisa had been incarcerated for years — who knew whether she'd survive out there in a world she couldn't know much about.

"Will you be all right?" Tracy asked, John making another attempt at freeing himself and failing. She clamped her inner thighs against his lower arms and hands — this bastard wasn't going anywhere.

"I'll manage. I've been let out sometimes, you know. I can shop and use a bank machine. He taught me to drive." Lisa paused. "Will *you* be all right?"

"Yes. I learnt to manage a long time ago. Go now, before the police come. They'll work out who *he* is and visit here. You need to be far away when that happens."

Lisa stood, and Tracy gazed up at her.

John let out a growl. "I'll tell them where you plan on going, you little bitch."

"Will you, John?" Tracy asked. "Will you really?"

Lisa spat on him then walked away. Her footsteps banged on the stairs — twelve in all — then she stopped. Tracy glanced over her shoulder, her leg muscles tiring from holding John in place.

"You might want to go to your boyfriend's after . . . after this," Lisa said. "I'm sorry."

Then she was gone, the door closing with a thud behind her.

John laughed, the sound throaty and mean, cracked and spiteful. "Your face!"

Tracy picked up the knife. "Not half as funny as yours."

Then she stabbed him in the gut, becoming her sister and *him* — two people she never wanted to be.

# CHAPTER TWENTY-SIX

Tracy yanked her phone out of John's pocket, ignoring his gurgles and the bubbles of blood spuming out of his mouth. Her phone in hand, she speed-dialled Damon, frantic for him to pick up so she could hear his voice. It rang, on and on. John grinned at her, his teeth red, his eyes shining.

He was a sick bastard, smug right up until the end.

"Is he dead?" she asked, thumping his chest. "Is Damon dead?"

"Only one . . . way to . . . find out," he spluttered, then coughed, blood spraying upwards.

She glared at him, remembering the scarf, her hiding in the wardrobe, and him not only defiling her, but working with her for years, hiding his identity all along.

She slit his throat as Lisa had done to Quinton — two murders with the same MO; Tracy wasn't taking the blame for this either. She climbed off him and ferreted around in a set of drawers beside the bed, finding a T-shirt. Back with John, she took off the glove and stuffed it in her front trouser pocket. The fingers dangled out. Then she pressed the shirt to John's neck wound, needing to make her attempt at saving him seem plausible — and she needed her clean hand to get blood on it.

A puddle of crimson grew around John's head, and a mini river flowed down a crack in a floorboard. Red fluid drizzled from his neck, his chest no longer rising and falling. She got up, backed away from him, and dialled Damon again. This time it went straight to voice mail.

"Damon, I'm coming. I know what's happened, so if you can hear me, sit tight."

She called Stuart next, babbling about John abducting her and taking her to her childhood home. There, she'd fallen asleep, only to wake and investigate, finding John in the basement. "I tried to save him, but he was already gone. I have to get to Damon's — he's not answering his phone, and John told me in the car on the way here that Damon's been hurt. I have to get to him. Send a car out to Damon's in case I don't get there quickly enough."

"All right, boss. I'll come out to secure John's scene with Mark — what's the address?"

She rattled it off then cut the call, sliding her phone away in her pocket, racing up the stairs and through the living room. She cursed herself, rushing back down to the basement to yank John's keys out of his pocket. On her way through again, she picked up the hateful scarf, then whipped into the garage. She shoved up the door then climbed into his car, dumping the scarf on the passenger seat, reversing out onto the drive then the street.

She'd killed a man and she didn't care. Her mind spinning with the events of the day, she put her foot down and sped towards Damon's, hoping to God he wasn't dead. She couldn't handle that — couldn't live with knowing he'd lost his life because of her; no, because of a man who'd thought he'd owned her.

Again, she made the journey without registering her surroundings, and screeched to a stop beside the post box, her headlights slicing through the darkness to illuminate a blue Ford in front. She left the engine running, too eager to get into the house. Out onto the pavement now, she was off and running, up the path to the front door. It stood open an inch, and she pushed inside, rushing into the hallway shouting, "Damon! Damon!"

At the living room door, she stopped short, gripping the jamb with one hand while flattening the other to her chest. Damon rested on his back on his cream rug, his face swollen and bruised, one eye more bloated and dark purple than the other. What the hell had happened to him? A white sheet had been draped over his midsection and chest, and rope bound his ankles. A red rose, placed across his stomach, and the rose petals leading from the door to him, had her knees buckling and bile streaking up into her mouth. Blood stained the sheet.

"Jesus Christ," she choked out, swallowing the burn.

She pushed the visual to the back of her mind and went to him, kneeling by his side to press two fingers to his pale neck, John's blood on them, flaking now, dark brown. A faint pulse fluctuated, and tears stung her eyes. She called an ambulance, giving the address, her name, and Damon's current condition. Putting the phone on speaker, she left it on the floor beside them so she could listen to the dispatcher's instructions. Even though she'd had training for this sort of situation, it had all fucked off and left her head.

She eased the sheet away to reveal a nasty gash in his stomach, blood drying on the outside, bright red and wet in the centre, still oozing out and down his side.

"He's bleeding," she said. "Possible knife wound."

"Press something to it — material, your hand," the woman on the phone said.

*I know this, for God's sake. Why can't I think for myself?*

Tracy grabbed a scatter cushion off the sofa. She pushed it against the gaping hole, and his eyelids flickered — somewhere in his unconsciousness, he still registered pain?

"How is his breathing, Tracy?"

"Shallow. Skin's clammy. He's lost a lot of blood. The police are meant to be on their way already — my colleague should have phoned it in. This is an officer down. We need help. Quickly!"

"The ambulance is around two minutes away — they're close because they've finished another call in the area, so you got lucky."

Tracy sighed with relief — she'd known it could have gone the other way, no ambulance available because of the shortages and the staff being stretched thin. She'd have hauled him out to the car somehow if she'd had to, but now she waited, her arms aching a little from her applying pressure.

Two minutes felt like twenty, but soon blue strobes streaked against the curtains, and footsteps clattered up the path. Tracy waited for one of the paramedics to take over dealing with Damon's wound, then she stepped back to give them space to work.

Not long after their arrival, the two-man crew had loaded Damon onto a stretcher and were on their way out.

"Will he be all right?" she asked, going to squeeze her bottom lip with a finger and thumb then stopping herself — the scent of John's blood had her stomach protesting.

"Think you got to him in time. The knife wound is thankfully in his stomach, can't see it being deep enough to have nicked any major organs, and as for his face . . . Appears to be a bad beating. Or," he leant over the stretcher, "possibly a boot — you can see the faint tread pattern on his skin."

Tracy's stomach nearly gave up its contents. "Dear God . . ."

"He's been lucky."

He turned to his colleague, and they wheeled Damon out and down the path. Tracy followed, standing beside the post box as they loaded Damon into the ambulance.

"I'll follow shortly," she said. Now she knew the odds of him surviving were good, she could afford a little time.

"He'll probably go into surgery pretty sharpish, so don't rush."

Tracy nodded.

The ambulance sped off, lights flashing, and she switched John's car off. Then she went into the house and collected a cloth from under the sink. She wiped every surface

Lisa might have touched throughout the house, including the front door, then grasped the clean handle from the outside to give credence to her having touched it when she'd come in.

With the place as free of her sister — still a shock she had one, still too much to take in — as she could get it, she left the house and, climbing into John's car, made her way to the hospital.

# CHAPTER TWENTY-SEVEN

Damon came out of surgery at five a.m. — he hadn't been taken to the operating theatre 'sharpish' as the paramedic had predicted. Accident and Emergency was full to the gills, and once Damon had been hooked up to blood and fluids, he'd stabilised, and although he'd been stabbed, the wound wasn't as bad as she'd feared.

She sat by his bed, Stuart, Mark, and Roger standing on the other side. She'd been through everything with them — minus John's involvement in the child abuse — while Damon still slept. She didn't want his wife and children tainted by the actions of that sick son of a bitch. Him abducting her was a bad enough pill for Brenda to swallow.

Over a good couple of hours, Tracy explained her life, *him*, and how the recent murders were tied. Roger had recorded her statement on his phone — it would save her repeating herself at some point in the future, and he could type it up later.

Exhausted, she looked up at the three men who had been her rocks, along with Damon, ever since she'd become a DI. They each had different expressions.

Mark — compassion.

Stuart — anger.

Roger — pity.

No. No, she couldn't have that.

"Do *not* feel sorry for me," she said. "I've moved on — I'm okay. Really, I'm okay." Tears fell, but they weren't for what her men probably thought.

She cried for the child she'd been, that little girl, innocent once. For Lisa, born first then shunned when a new victim had arrived — Tracy, the new baby. Lisa shoved away in a basement, only to be let out when Tracy had left home. Her mother — their mother — living with a man who'd 'loved' her babies more than he should, and wrecked her life with lie upon lie — including pretending her firstborn had run away.

Where had her mother been when John had visited Tracy and Lisa? Shopping? Tracy wanted to believe her mother had known all along, maybe too scared of *him* to speak out — even if it meant saving her children.

His manipulation skills were such that any scenario was plausible.

"So we're still on the hunt for the EFIT woman? Who *is* that?" Stuart asked.

Tracy shrugged. "Some woman he lived with, I assume. A girlfriend. We'll have to keep an eye out, obviously, but I'm guessing she's long gone. We'll continue searching, but don't be surprised if she doesn't surface. Would you, after maybe knowing the man you loved killed all those people?" *God forgive me for lying. Again.* "If she's caught, she'll probably end up in a hospital — her mind is, without question, a mess if she's been privy to all this. I feel sorry for her despite what she's done." She sighed. "I feel sorry for everyone involved. But not myself. If I do that, I'll break."

She stood. Walked around the bed to hug each of them, grateful for their support. She thought of something then, lifting her head from Mark's chest. She stepped back, dug into her pocket, and pulled out John's car keys.

"One of you will need to sort John's vehicle. There's a woollen scarf on the passenger seat. Don't let it go into evidence. Take it to Brenda, his wife. It belonged to their daughter — not sure which one."

Mark nodded. "All right, boss. You going home?"

"No, I'll stay here for a while — until Damon wakes up. Not like we have to worry about John being pissed off with us not turning up for work in" — she checked her watch; blood stain on the glass — three-quarters of an hour."

Stuart groaned. "I can't get over this. John, of all people. He was such a good man. It won't be the same at work without him."

*You have no idea . . . and be glad you don't.*

To stop the conversation going further, with more praise for John, the motherfucker, Tracy said, "Day off, lads. Go home. Get some sleep. I'll deal with any phone calls. I'll ring the station and ask the desk sergeant to forward everything to me."

* * *

Tracy spent the next few hours answering calls, verifying what had happened to DI Jacobs on the other team, and sleeping in the chair with her head on Damon's bed. It sounded cruel, but she was glad to hand everything over — this had been one hell of a ride, and because she'd been involved in a personal capacity, she could no longer work the case.

She hoped Lisa was never found.

Unless she had a penchant for killing and continued elsewhere. Then whoever apprehended her could throw the book at her.

Damon stirred, and she leant forward, eager to be the first person he saw. His good eye opened, the other resembling a ripped plum, and she could have wept. He was here, with her, and she wouldn't have to face life without him.

"You're fine," she said. "You're going to be fine."

She reached for the buzzer, pressed it for the nurse, and held his hand until someone came. He was allowed an ice chip, then the head end of his bed was raised so he could sit up after a fashion.

The nurse left, and a tear trickled down Damon's cheek.

"I . . . I wasn't scared for me," he said, voice raspy. "Just for you."

"I know," she said, squeezing his hand. "It's all over now. I'll tell you about it once you're up to hearing it. None of it is pretty, and it's almost exactly what I suspected."

He raised his eyebrows then grimaced.

"Yes, I had a feeling but didn't believe myself until close to the end," she said.

They sat quietly for a while until Damon dozed off again, so she rose and stretched the knots out of her muscles. She left his room and took the elevator to the basement, striding down the corridor that led to the morgue. That smell attacked her, and she resisted gagging, pinching her nose until she reached Kathy's office on the lower floor of the hospital.

Tracy peered through the porthole-style window in the top of the door. Kathy sat at her desk, typing on her keyboard. Tracy knocked, waited for Kathy to turn and beckon her to come in, then entered.

"So sorry to hear about your father and John," Kathy said. "I don't know what to say."

"You don't have to say anything. I'm glad they've gone."

"What?" Kathy frowned.

Tracy had wanted to open up about her childhood to Kathy but had never found the courage. What if Kathy had thought her dirty? Thought Tracy was somehow to blame for what *he'd* done? Maybe that was why their relationship had derailed — Tracy had never been truly honest about who she was and what she'd been through. She'd never given Kathy the chance to help her.

"I'll tell you about it another time — I'm all talked out regarding those two."

"Blimey, and there was me thinking you'd come down to see them."

"Oh, I've come down to see one of them, all right, and that's the man who called himself my father. I want to make sure he's really dead. I know John is; I tried to save him.

But the other? I want to see him for myself, so there's no questioning it. Besides, I'm his daughter. I can identify him."

Kathy eyed her warily. "Okay . . . If you're sure you can handle it."

"Of course. It's not like I'm going to break down and sob, is it?"

Kathy shrugged. "I'm really sorry about John, matey." She sighed. "Come on, then."

She followed Kathy into the main room that held the corpses.

"I'll deal with this one," Kathy said to her male assistant, who left on silent feet.

*Creepy sod.*

Tracy stood silently while Kathy found *his* drawer then pulled him out. He had the dignity of being covered with a white sheet, just like every other dead person, something he didn't deserve. Still, rules were rules, and whether he was a paedophile or not, he was treated the same.

"Do you want me to draw down the sheet?" Kathy asked.

"No, thank you. I'll be fine by myself, actually. You can wait outside or whatever. I'd like to be alone."

Kathy raised her eyebrows then left, the door swishing shut behind her.

Tracy hesitated revealing *his* face — why, she didn't know. She took a deep breath, dreading how she'd feel. She *thought* she'd be okay, that she was strong enough, but who knew how emotions would take her once his face was showing? Who knew what memories would slam into her, forcing her to her knees on the tiled floor, her heart and soul ripped open, leaving her vulnerable when she so wanted to be strong. She didn't love him — she hadn't for years, so . . .

She peeled the material back, and there *he* was, the man who'd ruined her, ruined her life, her sister's, her mother's, and God knew how many other children. The thought of that sent prickles of shame scratching through her, and his features blurred a little — damn it, she hadn't wanted to cry.

She hated him, and maybe one day that would pass, and she'd think of him as just some man she used to know, someone insignificant, one grain of sand on a beach, easily ignored.

She leant closer, until she was an inch from his face and his pores were visible, his stubble, the veins on the side of his nose. The shape of his nostrils — and she remembered how they'd flared when he'd loved her.

"You're an evil bastard," she said. "And I'm glad you're dead." She straightened. "Now *fuck* off to Hell where you belong."

She walked out, past Kathy, and said over her shoulder, "We should go for a drink, okay? I'll tell you a few things that might explain why I've been . . . a bitch to you."

"All right," Kathy said.

Tracy strode up the corridor, breathing in the odour of death this time — she never wanted to forget it, because every time she smelt it, she'd be reminded *he* was gone, burning in flames.

She made her way to a café on the ground-floor level and bought a coffee, immediately thinking of Dr Schumer. She'd never know whether he was on her side or *his*, but it didn't matter now.

Choosing a seat by the window, she gazed out over the hospital grounds, at people leaving the car park and scuttling inside out of the rain that fell steadily, at the buses drawing up to the stop to collect visitors of the sick.

And she realised life went on, regardless. The good path was ahead, the Past would fade, and she'd forever keep the secret that she'd killed John and let her sister go. And she'd try harder with Damon — God, how many times had she told herself to do that?

Some things never changed.

She still had all those lies.

**THE END**

## THE JOFFE BOOKS STORY

We began in 2014 when Jasper agreed to publish his mum's much-rejected romance novel and it became a bestseller.

Since then we've grown into the largest independent publisher in the UK. We're extremely proud to publish some of the very best writers in the world, including Joy Ellis, Faith Martin, Caro Ramsay, Helen Forrester, Simon Brett and Robert Goddard. Everyone at Joffe Books loves reading and we never forget that it all begins with the magic of an author telling a story.

We are proud to publish talented first-time authors, as well as established writers whose books we love introducing to a new generation of readers.

We won Trade Publisher of the Year at the Independent Publishing Awards in 2023. We have been shortlisted for Independent Publisher of the Year at the British Book Awards for the last four years, and were shortlisted for the Diversity and Inclusivity Award at the 2022 Independent Publishing Awards. In 2023 we were shortlisted for Publisher of the Year at the RNA Industry Awards.

We built this company with your help, and we love to hear from you, so please email us about absolutely anything bookish at: feedback@joffebooks.com.

If you want to receive free books every Friday and hear about all our new releases, join our mailing list: www.joffebooks.com/contact

And when you tell your friends about us, just remember: it's pronounced Joffe as in coffee or toffee!

## ALSO BY EMMY ELLIS

**DETECTIVE TRACY COLLIER**

Book 1: GUTTED

**DI BETHANY SMITH**

Book 1: THE COLD CALL KILLER
Book 2: THE CREEPY-CRAWLY KILLER
Book 3: THE SCREWDRIVER KILLER
Book 4: THE SCORCHED SKIN KILLER
Book 5: THE STREET PARTY KILLER
Book 6: THE CANDY CANE KILLER
Book 6.5: THE SECRET SANTA KILLER
Book 7: THE MEAT HOOK KILLER
Book 8: THE BLADE KILLER
Book 9: THE SLEDGEHAMMER KILLER

**DETECTIVE CAROL WREN MYSTERIES**

Book 1: SPITE YOUR FACE
Book 2: HOLD YOUR BREATH
Book 3: GUILT BURNS HOLES
Book 4: BEST SERVED COLD
Book 5: BLOOD RUNS DEEP

Printed in Great Britain
by Amazon

44914205R00101